TABLE OF CONTENTS

Welcome to Flat River

Come spend some time in Flat River, Nebraska, a small town filled with the strong men and women who settled the wild west of the Nebraska Plains, from 1860 to 1880. Flat River is home to unique characters, strong heroines, swoony heroes, and stories that will stand the test of time. All of these wholesome stories can be read by readers of all ages. They are filled with family values, romance, humor, and a sprinkle of faith.

Do you love wholesome romance, funny stories, and want a new recipe each week? Join Christine's newsletter and get a free copy of The Flat River Matchmaker, the prequel to the series of the same name.

https://bookhip.com/FPZDPSD

Thank You!

Thank you to Barb Hupp, Debbie Moody, and Jean Alfieri for coming up with character names at a moments notice! I appreciate you so much!

His Christmas Bride

All that widow Regina Graham wants to do is provide a home for her children. After being separated from their wagon train, they managed to go unnoticed along the banks of a nearby small creek. With harsh winter weather looming over them, she isn't sure how much longer they can survive. The last thing she expects is to be accused of trespassing by a large mountain man who scares her more than any winter storm ever could! With nowhere to go, and no way to survive, she can't imagine why a stranger would help her or her children or what he possibly wants in return.

Fur-trapper Joseph Moore can't believe someone has been stealing his traps, but he intends to get to the bottom of it one way or another. When the smell of roasted rabbit draws him to an abandoned line shack on the edge of his property, the last thing he expects to find is a terrified woman and her two small children hiding. Hungry and cold, Joseph knows they won't survive the approaching winter storm even if he allows them to stay. Left with no other choice, he takes them to his cabin to wait out the storm, with the intention of delivering them to the marshal in Flat River as soon as the weather clears. With Christmas fast approaching, Regina's two children prepare for the holiday and Joseph finds himself caught up in the excitement.

Determined to bring a bit of joy to a family who has lost so much, dare Joseph to hope for his own miracle. Can he make Regina *his Christmas bride*?

CHAPTER ONE

Flat River, Nebraska
December 1860

Joseph Moore guided his horse between the trees that ran along the river towards his cabin. The sound of his horse, Chestnut, breaking through the thin layer of ice coating the fluffy snow below, shattered the silence.

Thankfully, the snow wasn't over six inches deep, but he had heard in town that there was a nor'easter on the horizon. How the old-timers could tell by looking at the sky, Joe would never know, but they did.

"This one might bring a foot or more," they told him as he tucked his purchases into his saddlebags before heading back towards his small cabin tucked along the river.

Cold air filled his lungs, and with each breath, he exhaled white puffs. Leaning down to stroke his horse's neck, he reassured the beast in quiet tones. "Almost there, Chestnut."

The wind was picking up, rustling the bushes that lined the water's edge. A rabbit hopped out, and paused, its nose twitching for danger before hopping away further down the bank in search of a stray blade of grass that might poke through the icy shell. Joe chuckled as he turned up the collar on his coat and shrunk inside the wool to block some of the frigid gusts. The rabbit was so light that it didn't even break through the ice. It simply slid along the top towards its destination.

"Lucky for you, little fella," Joe called to the critter, "that I don't have my traps out this far, and you are too small for the stewpot."

Joe lived close to town, but considering that town was at least a mile, it still wasn't that close. He had his provisions for winter, but something was messing with his traps, and he needed to purchase some wire to secure them in place. He wasn't sure if it was an animal or another hunter that was dragging them off, but once he was done with them, there wasn't a man or beast that could walk off with one of Joe's traps again.

As a hunter and trapper, Joe's busy season was October through March. That is when the animals had thick pelts and fetched the highest price per pound. A good season would mean that he had money in the bank and food on his table for the following year. A poor season... well, he didn't want to think about what a poor season would mean.

So far, this year had been a very good season. At least, until his traps started disappearing a week ago.

Humming to himself to prevent his lips from turning numb, he rounded the last set of trees before he would make the brief climb towards his cabin. There were very few hills in Nebraska, but he was fortunate to stake his claim on one of them.

His land was shaped like a triangle, wide at the bottom and pointed at the top. The wide piece spanned over three hundred feet of river bottom and creek beds, which were perfect for hunting mink, rabbits, beavers, and muskrats. Inside the woods, he could find wildcats or foxes. If he was very fortunate, he might find a wolf, as buyers highly prized those pelts back east. A wolf's pelt could fetch nearly twenty dollars each.

As he reached the clearing, the wind stopped its low whistle, and he thought he heard an ax hissing in the air before pounding into a piece of wood. There wasn't anyone that lived close and the only cabin that Joe knew about was a tiny cabin sitting at the edge of the Chapman ranch. It was the cabin that the Chapmans first built when they arrived in town nearly twenty years prior.

Joe knew, because he grew up in an almost identical cabin further down the river, as he arrived on the same wagon train with his parents, his brother and his sister. His family quickly outgrew the small cabin and now Joe lived higher on the hills, surrounded by ponderosa pines in a small clearing. His brother Devin lived in a small cabin on the other side of the clearing. It was nice having family close, but not too close. *Five hundred yards was close enough.*

Chestnut's ears jerked at the sound of the ax once more.

There shouldn't be anyone using the cabin. After the Chapmans started building their home, the cabin was rented by the U.S. Marshal service. The Marshals would use it when they were traveling through the area. But Marshal Orrin Briggs had a place in town now, and Joe had just seen him an hour ago having coffee with Doc in the mercantile. Now it was a line rider's cabin, used for cowhands to escape the bitter weather when searching for wayward strays. It had fallen into disrepair as no one had time for the upkeep required.

Joe hadn't seen any indications of wayward cows or calves in the snow. Clicking his tongue, he guided his mount back into the woods towards the line rider's cabin.

Might as well investigate, he thought. I might even find out why my traps are going missing.

Chestnut didn't appear happy to be moving away from home and his warm barn. He snorted his displeasure.

"I agree, boy," Joe said, tucking further into his coat and wrapping the pelts tighter around his shoulders. He thought about the pot of coffee he left warming on the stove and hoped it wouldn't take too long before he could head back to his little cabin nestled in the woods.

Joseph was convinced that there was a trespasser as the scent of burning pine rose through the air, punctuated by roasting meat. *Rabbit*, if he wasn't mistaken. As they closed the distance, the sound of the ax became louder. It wasn't a steady ribbon of sounds, more of a hit and miss, peppered by light grunts.

He broke through the clearing and stopped short as he spied a small figure bent over to lift a piece of wood and place it back on the stump.

The person hadn't seen him yet, so he stood at the corner of the trees and watched them for a moment. When they stood upright, he realized it was a woman, not very tall, and completely not dressed for the weather. She lacked a hat and any type of proper coat. Instead, a thin gray shawl wrapped around her shoulders, and crossed over her front, before being tucked into a brown skirt that was covered in patches of different calicos. Dark brown hair, flattened from the heavy snow, stuck to her skin. Ungloved hands pushed the wet strands away with blue fingers, revealing skin that was mottled red from the cold. Joe could see white clouds form as she took a deep breath before reaching down to pick up the wood, exposing worn boots held together by string wrapped around the toes.

She lifted the ax once more over her head and brought it down with all her might. The wood split into two pieces, and Joe chuckled as she did a little dance in the snow.

The woman was not from around here. There was no way Ingrid or Weston Chapman would allow someone to just live in their cabin and not make sure the person at least had their basic needs taken care of. He nudged Chestnut forward and cleared his throat to make the woman aware of his presence. The woman spun around with a shriek, her skirt trapping her legs as she stumbled forward with the wood in her hands. She let loose another loud scream as she fell towards the ground with a thud.

Joe slid off the horse and released Chestnut's reins, rushing to the woman in three enormous steps. Kneeling in the snow, not caring about the cold seeping through the wool covering his legs, he grabbed the woman by her shoulders and gently lifted her up, brushing the ice, mud, and debris from her shawl.

"Are you alright?" he asked, concern evident on his face.

The woman took deep breaths, the cold rattling in her chest. She nodded, unable to speak, her eyes wide as she took in his appearance. Joe gave another chuckle. He probably looked like a grizzly bear, coming off the horse and approaching her with furs covering his shoulders. He, unlike the woman beneath his gloved hands, knew what the weather could do to a person if it caught them unaware.

The spring and summers in Flat River, Nebraska, were pleasant enough. The fall temperatures were cool, but winter could turn on a dime and Joe had heard of more than one man freezing because they were ill prepared. That is why there were cabins up and down the Platte

River. But this cabin was in no such shape to be lived in.

"I'm not going to hurt you," he said gruffly. "I just want to make sure you're alright."

Leaning back on her heels, she put a hand on her chest and held her arm across her belly. Closing her eyes for a moment, Joe watched as a lone tear rolled down her cheek. She lifted a shaky hand and wiped at her cheek before opening her eyes to look at him.

He sucked a breath between his teeth as golden eyes peered beneath dark lashes. They reminded Joe of the wild cats he would hunt in the deepest winter. Fat snowflakes framed her face, and a few twigs and leaves were caught in her unruly dark locks. Joe's fingers itched to reach and pull the branches from its tangled nests, but he released her and curled his fingers tightly in his palm.

He could feel his knee throbbing from the dampness encompassing his joint.

"I hurt my arm when I fell." Her voice was so soft, he had to strain his ears to hear it.

"Let's get you inside," Joe offered. It wouldn't do him any good to be sitting around in wet pants, either. His trapping business didn't take a day off, and Joe couldn't afford to be sick.

"No, that's alright, I can manage."

Joe rolled back on his heels and stood in one motion, pulling her up with him. She was no bigger than a church mouse. Her head reached halfway up his chest and his arms could swallow her if he was so inclined to pull her into them.

He was.

Just to keep her warm, he thought.

"I don't think so." He turned her around and guided her towards the cabin. "Your teeth are chattering. I'll bring in the wood and finish chopping the rest for you."

"You don't have to do that, honestly. I don't want to accept charity from strangers."

"You know you aren't supposed to be here, don't you, ma'am?" He winced as another tear rolled down her face.

"The cabin looked abandoned."

"How long have you been here?" The woman didn't answer. Joe repeated the question, this time his voice coming out like a growl. The woman jumped and glanced at the door. "I told you I won't hurt you. This is my neighbor's cabin. My property is that way." He pointed past the trees. "Town is that way. Why aren't you in town?"

"I went to town when we arrived in the summer."

"The summer? So," Joe counted on his fingers, "you've been here at least six months?" The woman nodded. Joe ran his hand down his face. "Ma'am, right now I'll accept a hot cup of coffee. There aren't too many strangers in this part. We got to look out for each other."

"I-I don't have any coffee."

"No coffee?"

The woman shook her head. "I can make you some pine needle tea, though. It's hot. I don't have any sugar."

Joe tried not to grimace.

"Where's your man?"

The woman rubbed her hands under her arms and hopped from one leg to another. "He's out hunting. Went to find a deer."

Joe knew she was lying — no man would drink

pine needle tea of his own free will. "Uh-huh." He headed back towards his horse. "Why would he be going hunting for deer when I can smell that you're roasting a rabbit?"

"I need to get my wood. You can git along now." Joe heard the ice crunch under her worn boots as she scrambled to pick up the fallen sticks.

"I'm just grabbing coffee." He rustled inside the saddle pack and pulled out a small sack of coffee beans. He didn't know if the woman even had a grinder. "You get inside and brew up these beans, and I'll get the rest of the wood chopped." He knew he wasn't going to let her stay in the cabin alone. He had heard Weston say more than once that the chinking needed to be repaired. If a good gust came through, it would blow this woman from one end of the cabin to the other. Joe held the bag out towards her. "Once I'm done, we can have a chat about what you are doing out here."

"I'd rather not."

Joe dropped the bag to his side and scratched his chin. The growth, which kept the cold from biting his skin, was covered in frost. He couldn't imagine how chilled her skin must be. "Well, I suppose I could ride over to the Chapmans and ask if they know they have an interloper on their land. They just might throw you out in the snow. Shame with a storm coming." The woman's eyes went wide. "Or I suppose I could just mosey back into town, get a new sack of coffee, let the marshal know that someone is staying in his old cabin and is a thief as well."

"A thief?"

"Yuuuup." Joe drawled out the word, long and slow. "Those look like my missing traps on the porch. And judging by the smell of the rabbit you're cooking, I'd venture to say they were full when you pulled them from under the brush."

"Oh, please don't. I'm not causing any trouble."

"They don't take kindly to thieving around here, Miss...," Joe paused, hoping she'd provide her name.

"Mrs." She looked like she might burst into tears. "Mrs. Regina Graham."

"Mrs. Graham. Mrs. Graham." Joe rolled the name around on his tongue. "Why does that name sound familiar?"

"We came to town on the wagon train."

Joe's eyebrows arched in surprise. "Your husband was ill."

"Yes. He died."

"I'm sorry to hear that. Why didn't you leave with the rest of the wagons?"

Regina jutted her chin out and swiped angrily at her cheek. "They don't want a widowed woman traveling with them without a man."

"I see," Joe said, rubbing his bottom lip. He didn't. Anger brewed up in his chest. Why would a group of God-fearing people leave a woman to fend for herself in the wilderness? He had to admire the spunky creature in front of him. She had survived creek-side for nearly six months, with no one noticing her. That took a certain amount of gumption.

"What are you going to do, Mr….?" She arched a brow back at him.

Joe grinned. "Moore. Joseph Moore, at your service, ma'am. You can call me Joe. Let me chop you some wood. You get inside and get warm. Eat your supper and we'll figure this out. I'd like to get out of the cold before the snow really falls."

The creaking of the front door drew his attention back to the broken porch. A small boy, only four or five years old, peeked his head outside.

"Mama? You comin'? It's awful cold in here."

Joe swallowed as he looked from the small child to the woman who moved between him and the door to protect her offspring.

Things just became a lot more complicated.

CHAPTER TWO

Gina stood on the edge of the porch holding the leather harness of a worn-out mare as she watched Joe place the giant fur that wrapped around his shoulders on top of her small children.

He was a bear of a man. In fact, that is exactly what she thought he was when he entered the clearing. All she saw was a dark brown furry object approaching her. That the bear was riding a horse didn't matter. *Perhaps bears rode horses in Nebraska.* Being from South Carolina, Gina realized she was naïve about several things.

Especially how the good Christian women of

the South Carolina to Oregon wagon train treated her once her husband died.

They just left her!

Leaving her and her children behind to perish. They didn't want an unmarried woman, even if she was grieving, tempting their husbands on the rest of the trip west. At least they didn't take her wagon. Gina had heard stories of women being abandoned with nothing but a small sack of supplies. She didn't want to believe the stories because they sounded too horrible to be true.

Until they left her behind.

They left her food; but they did, however, take her water barrels and oxen since she wouldn't need them. Or at least that is what they said. They left her a horse, with a back so bowed, that Gina was afraid to put a saddle on it or use the animal to pull a wagon to town.

She remembered standing with her children, alongside the unmarked grave of her husband as she watched the wagons slowly roll out of Flat River back towards the main trail. Once her tears were dry enough to allow her to see, they followed the creek until they came across the deserted shack nestled in a cluster of tall pines. Gina was thankful that the horse could pull the wagon as far as it did.

Bethany's lyrical voice brought her out of her memories. She looked down from the porch to see Joe's large hands gently tucking the edges of the fur under the many layers of blankets that she had already piled on top of them. "That should keep you warm."

"Is it far to where we are going?" Thomas asked, his blue eyes wide as he took in the giant of a man.

Joe shook his head. "Not too far. About twenty-minutes. Might take a little longer with the wagon."

It didn't take much for him to convince Gina that she needed to move from the cabin. Not because they didn't have permission, but for the health of her children. Thomas's chest was rattling, and she knew her son would get sicker the colder the cabin became.

The remnants of their old Conestoga sat behind the small cabin. Gina had already burned the wooden bows for firewood, but she couldn't bring herself to tear apart the wagon just yet. She wasn't that desperate.

Perhaps she was, if she was taking help from this stranger and now packing up her children to take them to his home in God knows where. If she found him scary when he entered the clearing, his entire demeanor changed once Thomas had opened the door.

She saw anger, confusion, fury, and sadness cross his handsome face, but he was as patient as Job as he made coffee over the open fire and allowed the children to eat the pilfered rabbit without a word. When they were done, he hitched his own horse to the front of the wagon and loaded what was left of Gina's meager belongings into the wagon.

"What do you want to do with Lucy?" Gina asked, lifting the harness.

"We'll tie her on the back. She's not good for much right now," Joe said, eyeing the ribs protruding from the sides of the horse. "But with some good feed, she can do some light work for you by spring."

"The wagon master told me to just let her go once I was done with her."

Joe's brow furrowed. "The Indians would make quick work out of her. Just tie her up at the back."

"What do you mean?"

"A horse would feed a village for at least a week."

Gina gasped. "I—you mean—I would never."

"Just tie her up and let's go. The temperature is dropping." Joe moved around to the front of the wagon and checked the straps on his horse.

She felt his eyes bore into her back as she walked around and tied the mare to the back of the wagon. She patted Lucy on her soft muzzle and leaned her head against her neck. "I'm sorry, girl. I would never let you be eaten," she whispered. Why did David have to leave her alone? She looked at the sky, heavy with dark clouds, and exhaled. *Please Lord*, she thought. *Just let us be safe.*

"Mama?"

Stroking the horse's neck, she turned to look at her daughter. "What is it, darling?"

"Don't cry, Mama." Bethany's voice was

muffled under the warm fur. "He's a good man."

"How do you know that, child?"

"I heard him praying by the fire. Daddy used to pray by the fire and Daddy was a good man."

Gina gave a half gasp, half laugh, and wiped her tears away. "Yes, your Daddy was."

"Mama?"

"What is it, Thomas?"

"Do you think we can still celebrate Christmas if we aren't here?"

Gina's heart cracked a little. Her children had been talking about Christmas. Even though it was still two weeks away, Thomas was excited about the prospect of a proper Christmas feast. She wished she shared her son's enthusiasm, but if she resorted to stealing rabbits to feed them, she didn't know how she was going to prepare a Christmas feast.

"I'm sure we can, love."

Walking to the side of the wagon, she stood on her toes and leaned over to make sure the children were settled between the boxes and blankets. Looking at her meager belongings, she wondered where she would end up after the storm. "You children snuggle down and hold each other tight. I don't know if it will be a bumpy ride or not." Kissing her fingertips and pressing it to each child's forehead, she then moved to the front of the wagon. "Do you want me to walk?"

Joe's eyes flickered over the back of his horse at her. He was adjusting the harness and grunted before placing his arms on top of the animal.

"No. Especially not in those boots. You climb up there and wrap yourself in that blanket. Make sure the children are alright. I'll walk."

"I—"

"Don't argue, woman, just get on the wagon. We need to get out of here." He grabbed the reins and moved to the front of the horse.

Gina scrambled on top of the wagon bench and wrapped herself in the quilt, thankful for the warmth that it provided. The wagon lurched forward, and she grasped the edge of the bench, the wood rough under her fingertips. Her fingers were so stiff from the cold, she flexed them before grabbing the edge of the quilt and using it in place of gloves. It hadn't been cold enough on the journey west to need gloves and what little yarn she had, she used to knit each of the children a pair of mittens for Christmas. At least they would have something in their sock on Christmas morning.

As the wagon made its way from the clearing, Gina took advantage of the slow pace to study Joe. He dressed in a long dark duster that was scuffed from wear. On top of his head, he had a leather hat that did nothing to protect his ears from the cold. She winced, thinking that he sacrificed his own comfort to make sure that her children were warm.

He glanced back at her with a smile, and she felt her knees knock under the quilt.

It's just the cold, she told herself.

But she knew it wasn't.

She knew he had rich brown hair as he had taken off his hat in the small cabin. It reminded Gina of the beans he used to make coffee before they left on their slow trek up the hill. His eyes were lighter, with gold rings in the center. She had never seen such beautiful eyes on a man before. An unkept beard covered his chin, but she supposed that there wasn't much use for grooming out here in the middle of nowhere. At least his clothes were clean, and he appeared to have bathed in the past month.

What she would give for a warm bath and a bar of soap.

"There's a bathhouse," he replied gruffly.

"Excuse me?" Gina sat up on the bench.

"I said there is a bathhouse where we are going. Can't say that there is any soap other than what my Ma makes, but it will get you clean. I used it two days ago."

Gina felt her cheeks flush. "Did I say that out loud?"

He looked back over his shoulder and his cheeks lifted. She leaned back and placed her fingers against her chest, sucking in a breath. David had been handsome, but this man was … *breathtaking*. She hoped she wasn't being rude by staring at him.

"You did." He gave a little chuckle.

"Do you live with your Ma?" The thought gave Gina comfort that there might be a woman there.

"No. She and Pa live in a house in the next clearing over. It is just me and my brother where I am."

"Your brother?"

Joe nodded and guided the horse away from the line of trees to a path that ran along the creek. "Yes. His name is Devin. He lives in a house on the other side of the clearing."

Gina watched the water rush around snow-covered rock towards its destination. A bird would flit down from one bush and land on the water's edge for a drink before spreading its wings to disappear into the branches above. *Oh, to be as free as a bird. They don't worry about where they lay their head at night, or where their next meal is coming from.*

"I think the actual verse is, Look at the birds of the air, for they neither sow nor reap nor gather into barns; yet your heavenly Father feeds them. Are you not of more value than they?"

She gave an awkward laugh. "I guess I should stop talking to myself."

"Or at least talking out loud."

"You know your Bible, Mr. Moore."

"Call me, Joe. My Ma would read it to us every

night before bed. It was her most valuable possession on the trip out west."

"What's your wife going to say when you bring home a woman and two children?"

"Don't know."

Apprehension filled Gina's chest. What would she say if David brought home a woman and two children? She didn't know. The good Christian thing would be to share what they had, but she didn't know how she felt about sharing her home or husband with another woman, even if it was just temporary.

"I promise we won't be a burden."

Joe leaned over and patted the horse's neck. "I don't know because I don't have a wife." Relief flooded through Gina. "Where are you from, Mrs. Graham?"

"South Carolina." She pulled the quilt tighter around her. "It wasn't this cold there."

Joe threw his head back and let out a guffaw that echoed across the trees. "It will be a lot colder here in January."

She glanced at the back of the wagon. Her

children had fallen asleep under the heavy fur. She envied them. They could fall asleep anywhere. The cold was making her sleepy as well. She held onto the wagon bench and closed her eyes, allowing the gentle rhythm of the wagon to rock her. She thought of a large house filled with laughter, and hymns being sung around the fireplace. She had been looking forward to her first Christmas out west, in her new home, with her husband and children.

But all her dreams were just that ... *dreams*.

She must have dozed off, as she woke to large, fat flakes of snow falling on her cheeks. They weren't cold and wet like the previous snows. These flakes were dry, fat and sticking to everything. She fluttered her eyes, shaking the flakes from her lashes. Joe's hat had a thin covering of white, as did his shoulders.

Even the horse's mane was frosted in icy white. She brushed the snow from the bench and turned around to look at the children. They were still asleep. Looking around, she realized they were no longer near the river, as she couldn't hear water. Tall pine trees gently shook, sending showers of white down upon them. She was thankful the snow wasn't heavy.

"How much further?" she called to Joe. She wasn't sure how long she had been dozing.

"Not much. Just through those trees there." The horse was straining under the weight of pulling the wagon through the deepening snow. It must be nearly a good eight inches. Gina couldn't see Joe's boots as he pushed his way through, encouraging the horse with each step.

Soon she spied the clearing between the trees. As the horse broke through, she gave a gasp as two log cabins appeared with a barn built halfway between them. The cabins were identical and on opposite sides of the clearing. Made of rough hand-hewed wood, with mud and moss between logs, the cabins appeared to be sturdy and *warm*. A single plume of smoke rose from each cabin.

"Which one is yours?" Gina asked, lifting herself up further on the bench.

"The closest one."

The door to the cabin opened, and a tall man walked out. "I was wondering where you were. I didn't see your horse when I went to feed the animals, so I thought I better add wood to the … Jumpin' Jehoshaphat, Joe. What do you have there? Is that a woman?"

"Devin, this is Regina Graham. She and her two children will stay here for a bit."

"Staying here?"

Joe nodded, handing his brother the reins. "Yes. They'll stay in my cabin."

Gina watched as Devin scratched his chin before taking the leather straps.

"She will, uh-huh? And where will you be staying?"

"I'll be staying with you."

CHAPTER THREE

Joe knocked on the door to his cabin and kicked the snow off his boots, before pushing his way in. It was awkward knocking on his own door, but he wanted to afford Gina and her children at least a measure of privacy. She rushed to hold open the door for him, as he entered carrying a bucket of fresh milk and another with eggs.

"Good morning, Joe," she said cheerfully, closing the door behind him. "I said you didn't have to knock. This is your house, after all."

"Appreciate it, ma'am, but I'll knock just the same." He placed the buckets on the table and looked around. "Did you sleep well?"

"I haven't slept properly since David died. I think it was the fear of being alone. But I finally fell asleep last night for the first time. At least I didn't hear the wind."

"I hope you are finding the house to your liking?"

Gina clasped her hands together and swung around. "It is beautiful and so much warmer than the cabin by the creek. I appreciate your hospitality and generosity."

Joe swallowed. He didn't have time to look at her yesterday as his anger overtook him at a group of settlers just leaving Gina and her children to survive on their own. He couldn't see past his own rage. Her face was freshly washed, and although her skin was still red from the wind, he could see that she had a smattering of freckles across her nose.

Her lips, no longer swollen and chapped, were the color of ripe berries that grew by the creek in summer. She was tinier than he first thought, now that she wasn't hidden under so many layers. He'd bet she weighed no more than a church mouse.

"When was the last time you had a decent meal?"

She moved to the fireplace and grabbed the arm holding a coffeepot over the fire with her apron. "I've not wanted to use many supplies, as I have no way of repaying you."

She placed the pot on the table as Joe grabbed two cups from the pegs on the wall.

"That wasn't the question I asked," he hissed, taking the pot from her and pouring the coffee into the cups before placing the pot on the table.

"I made sure the children ate first."

"Sit." It wasn't a request.

She slid into the chair and ran her fingers through her hair, the long tresses caressing her shoulder. He clenched his jaw so tightly that pain radiated up behind his eyes as he looked at her.

"I didn't mean to make–"

Joe held up his hand. "Just stay there. Where are the children?"

Her eyes darkened as she looked at him. "They are still asleep. I put them in your bed last night. They didn't even get out of their clothes."

Taking off his coat, he put it on the peg by the door and rested his hat on top of it.

He would bet his favorite hat she hadn't had a decent meal since she found the cabin. He wasn't trapping during the summer. There wasn't a point. If he or Devin wanted fresh meat, they could just go hunting with a long rifle. He wondered if Gina even knew how to hold a rifle. He didn't recall seeing her put one in the wagon when they were gathering her supplies. In fact, he didn't recall her putting much in the wagon.

He glanced at the snow melting into a puddle on the floor. Normally it wouldn't bother him, but for a moment he thought about apologizing for the mess, then he stopped.

Why should he? This was his house. A little melted snow never bothered him before.

He looked back at Gina, who was cupping the enamel mug. "Do you know how to make biscuits?"

Gina smiled. "I do. David said my biscuits were the best..." She looked downward. "I'm sorry. I shouldn't talk about him."

Joe walked over to the fireplace and kneeled to

move some coals to the side. Taking a cast-iron skillet with three legs, he rubbed the inside with his shirtsleeve before placing it over the coals to warm.

"You can talk about him. I don't mind." *He minded.* He didn't want to hear about the man who caused this woman to starve in the middle of Flat River. He rolled back on his heels and went to a door off to the side of the great room. "Supplies are in here," he said, opening the door. Tapping on the door next to it, he looked at her. "This one is a small root cellar. It has vegetables, some meat, and I normally put the milk in there."

Gina rose and walked over to the pantry. She stood next to him and surveyed the large barrels on the floor and the jeweled jars of preserves and other delights that his Ma made from the summer fruits. Joe leaned forward just slightly and closed his eyes, the scent of sunshine and earth filling his nostrils.

This David was one lucky man to have been married to a woman like Gina. She was beautiful, put the survival of her children before herself and Joe couldn't wait to taste the biscuits she would make for breakfast.

"I haven't seen a pantry this full before," she exclaimed, turning to look at Joe. Her mouth dropped in a silent *Oh*, and she stepped backwards, her back pressing against the doorframe. He was close enough to count the freckles on her nose. She had at least a dozen. He leaned over her, his arm grazing the side of her head as her breath quickened.

Her cheeks turned scarlet, deepening the windburn of her porcelain skin. A small pink tongue darted out and licked her lip before disappearing. Joe silently groaned at the sweetness and closed his eyes. Every hair on his head stood on end and his skin flamed as if he was standing next to the fireplace, not across the room.

She felt it too.

He knew he needed to break the moment. She was his guest. At least until they could get to town, and he could let Marshal Briggs know they were in trouble.

Taking a burlap sack from the wall, he stepped backwards. "Take what you need, but this is all I have for winter. I can't get more until Spring, so you must ration it. Bowls are over there." Leaving her at the door, he moved to the table and pulled out a large slab of bacon from the bag. Cutting thick slices with his hunting knife, he watched as Gina gathered up the items that she needed to make biscuits and placed them on the table.

"Should I use this milk?" she asked, pointing to the bucket he brought in.

"Unless you want the children to drink that. There is some milk that has the cream skimmed off in the root cellar."

"Do you have a clean pitcher? I can strain this."

Joe grunted and pointed to the root cellar. "On the pegs in there."

Gina returned with the pitcher of milk for the biscuits and an empty pitcher she used to strain the fresh milk for the children. They worked in silence as she rolled out the biscuit dough, and Joe placed the strips of bacon in the spider skillet. She carried the Dutch oven with the biscuits over to him and kneeled next to the fireplace.

Scooping coals on top of the Dutch oven, Gina asked softly, "Why do you and your brother live in separate houses?"

His lips turned up slightly. "That's an odd question."

"I just figured that you'd share a house. It would be less work."

Joe gave her a slight smile. "We're brothers." He shifted on the balls of his boots so he could look at her in the fire's glow. "We get along, but too much time in each other's company and we'd probably destroy everything in the house."

"You mean like fighting?"

He laughed. "I told you. We're brothers." Rolling back on his heels, he stood and offered his hand to Gina. "It will take a bit for the biscuits to cook, and I moved the bacon away from the fire. Let's go back to the table. I can monitor it there."

She eyed his outstretched palm for a moment before sliding her small hand into it. He curled his fingers around hers and pulled her up. She flew into his embrace when he yanked her arm with more force than he intended.

As her small body pressed against him, his arms wrapped around her waist to steady her. His heart started beating wildly, and he forgot to breathe for a minute as her hands grasped his shirt.

Her fingers dug into his muscles, which twitched under her touch as she looked at him, her eyes widening.

He saw her breath hitch. It would be so easy to lower his head and...

"Mama?" A small voice broke into his thoughts. "Why are you hugging, Mr. Moore?"

Gina jumped out of Joe's arms as if she had been burned.

Perhaps it was the fire, but she doubted it.

Flexing her fingers so she wouldn't reach back out and touch him, she gave him a quick glance. He was close enough that she could see his eyes softening as he looked at her. His jaw was clenched, and a slight tic pulsed in his cheek. She closed her eyes briefly, allowing the faint scent of the barn and burning wood to wash over her, before turning her attention to Bethany, who was standing barefoot in the middle of the room.

"He was just helping me up from the floor, sweetheart, and I lost my balance." She strode over and placed her hands on Bethany's shoulders, leading the young girl back to the table. "You need to put on your shoes. I don't want you to catch a cold."

"Can I have some milk first?"

"Let me find the glasses."

Joe pushed away from the fireplace. "I'll get them." He went to a cupboard and returned with two mugs that had seen better days. They were dented, but they worked. "I don't get much company," he said with a slight shake of his shoulders. "Where are your boots? In the bedroom?"

Bethany nodded as she took a large gulp of milk from the mug.

Joe returned a moment later and put the boots on the floor next to Bethany.

"Is Thomas still asleep?" Gina asked.

"His cough doesn't sound good. It would probably be a good idea to get Doc out to look at him."

"I'll take care of him." She didn't have money for a doctor.

"Give me your foot, honey," Joe said. Gina watched as he gently put on Bethany's boots and laced them. His large fingers fumbling with the bows. "Your Mama is right. It is too cold to be walking around without shoes."

"Thank you, Mr. Moore," Bethany said between sips of her milk.

"Just call me Joe." He ruffled her hair and went to check on the bacon as Gina fetched a jar of preserves from the pantry.

"Joe?" Bethany's voice squeaked.

"Bethany, right?"

"Yes. And my brother is Thomas." She slid from the chair and went over to watch Joe next to the fireplace. "We were talking last night." Gina's ears perked up. She thought her children were asleep. "We were wondering if Santa would know where we were since we didn't get to Oregon, and now we aren't in that cabin."

Joe scratched his chin. "I don't know much about Santa, darling."

The young girl clasped her hands together and swung from side to side. "Oh, I heard stories about him from books. He delivers gifts to children on

Christmas Eve if they put their socks by the chimney." She suddenly stopped swinging and cast her eyes towards the fire. "But he doesn't know where we are now."

Gina sat in a chair and wiped her eyes on her sleeves. The children were so excited about Christmas and had been talking about it for weeks. She didn't have the heart to tell them that Christmas on the prairie was going to differ from Christmases back home with their grandparents. She didn't even know where they would live once Joe took her to town to see the Marshal.

Why did David have to die?

"How do you celebrate Christmas, Joe?"

"There aren't many families around here. So, everyone gathers on Christmas Eve and has a meal and reflects on the meaning of Christmas together."

"Why Christmas Eve?" Gina asked. "Why not Christmas?"

"There is only one preacher that visits several small towns. He'll be here this year. He arrives on Christmas Eve. Since we don't have a church built yet, we normally meet in the Chapman's barn. It eventually became that all the families brought something to share, and we eat and visit together. Marmee, that's Ingrid Chapman, reads from the Bible and the preacher leads the service. Then we go home. Sometimes there might be a wedding or two. We spend Christmas day with our respective family."

"Doesn't Santa bring you anything?"

Joe let loose a little laugh. "No honey, he doesn't. We might get gifts from our parents, but not Santa."

"Oh. Well, I don't think that Mama can bring us what we want." Bethany wrinkled her face. "I don't think it will fit in a stocking either."

"Why's that?"

"Thomas and I want a Daddy."

Joe fell backwards on his heels and scrambled to a standing position. "You're correct, darling. That won't fit in a stocking." Looking at Gina, his eyes were hard. "I should go. The bacon is almost done. I'll bring back a chicken that you can stew for supper. The broth will be good for Thomas. My Ma said chicken broth cures everything."

"What about your biscuits?"

Joe pulled on his coat and opened the door. "Perhaps next time."

CHAPTER FOUR

"It's not funny." Joe slammed his mug on the table, causing hot liquid to splash over the side, burning his skin. "Ouch," he cried, lifting his hand to his mouth to soothe the burn. Glaring at his brother, who was now cackling, Joe narrowed his eyes once more. "I told you, it's not funny."

"I think it is, brother." Devin pinched the bridge of his nose, then wiped tears from his eyes. "I've not had a good laugh in a while." Standing, he slapped his brother on the shoulder. "Thanks for that."

"Where are you going?"

"I'm going to go deliver a chicken to that nice widow." Devin shrugged into his coat. "If those children want a Pa, and you aren't interested, there isn't any reason I shouldn't court her."

Joe pushed back from the table. "You stop that right now."

"Ah! You are interested."

"Am not."

"Are too." Devin's face split in a huge grin. "And stop sulking. Your face is going to freeze that way." With a laugh, he opened the door. "You coming? Or are you going to sit there and pout?"

Joe growled and pushed away from the table. Finishing his coffee in a large gulp, he grabbed his coat and followed Devin outside. His brother was two years older than Joe, just turning ten when they moved to the small town of Flat River. Now thirty years old, he knew Devin wanted to settle down. Unfortunately, women were few, so it shouldn't surprise Joe that his brother would take advantage of having a beautiful woman so close.

Then why did the thought of Devin touching Gina make his blood boil?

He shuffled his feet through the snow to the

chicken coop. Devin had already made quick work of selecting and culling an older hen that was no longer laying eggs. It was the very hen that Joe had identified earlier that morning.

"Have you noticed any others destined for the stew pot?" Joe asked.

"Maybe that one there," Devin said. "We should have more chicks come spring. That speckled one gets broody. We could probably have chicks if we force them into the barn."

Joe looked at the sky. The snow was coming down in fat flakes. "They might stay in there if the snow is deep enough."

Devin moved over to the front of the barn and started cleaning the bird. "You can take this to her in a few minutes. She'll have to remove the pin feathers, but it will cook up right nice."

Joe glowered at his brother. "I thought you were taking it over."

"No. I'll give you a chance to get your head on straight."

"I need to take her to see the Marshal."

"Why?" Devin rested the chicken on his knee.

"Because she was staying in some dilapidated line shack? Because she stole your traps?"

"The Marshal will know what to do with her."

"Joseph, sometimes you are as dumb as a bucket of rocks. You know what the Marshal is going to say? That she can get on the next wagon train headed West and she'll end up working in a bordello somewhere to support those kids. Or she'll have to go back east if that is even an option. Third choice is she finds a reputable man to marry." Devin gave a snort. "Once word gets out that there's a lady available, she'll be gobbled up like Ma's chicken supper." He started pulling out feathers once more. "Know what are even fewer out here? Women. We have a wagon stop in town for the doctor maybe once every what—three years? Not too many women on those trains, and less want to stay in this small town. Seems this might be something God had planned. You ever think of that?"

Joe dragged his toe in the snow until he uncovered the frozen dirt below, then he watched the fat flakes cover up the dark ground once more. "I am not dumb."

Devin finished plucking the chicken and dunked it in a bucket of cold water. "Is that what you took from the conversation?" Thrusting the cold hen towards his brother, he wiggled the naked bird. "Here. Go give it to your lady friend."

"She's not my lady friend. I just rescued her from the storm."

Wiggling the bird once more, Devin scowled. "I think you are protesting too much. Now git." Joe grabbed the bird by the legs and stomped back towards his cabin. "If she invites us for dinner, tell her I will gladly accept for both of us. I could use a home cooked meal."

Joe didn't turn around. Instead, he allowed the words his brother spoke to churn through his mind. What Devin said was true. There weren't many wagons that came through town. There were even fewer women. Why was he so against even entertaining the prospect of inviting Gina to stay?

Because he had known her for less than forty-eight hours.

She was still mourning her husband.

There were two children involved.

What if they weren't right for each other? He

didn't want to be in a miserable marriage for the rest of his life.

But what if they were?

He thought about what his Ma would say. He didn't need to ask; he knew. She'd tell him to pray about it. Jumping onto the porch, he stomped his boots to release the snow as the door opened.

"I saw you walking towards the house," Gina said. Her cheeks were flushed from working near the fire. "I still have biscuits left over from this morning, and the coffee is fresh. Would you like to come in?"

Joe held out the chicken in one hand as he stared at her. She had brushed her hair, and it tumbled in thick, soft waves around her shoulders. She had changed from the dress she wore that morning into a deep blue day dress which enhanced her gentle beauty.

"I—" He stared some more.

"Can you speak?"

He had words, they were just tied up with his tongue.

"Here's a chicken," he said, thrusting the naked

bird into her hands.

Perhaps Devin was right. He was dumber than a bucket of rocks.

Gina's face spread into a smile that sent his heart racing. The steady rush of blood drummed in his ears, and he was sure that she could hear it if she just leaned forward. Her lips moved, but he couldn't hear it over the pulsing of his heart.

"What?" he asked.

Gina grabbed his coat and pulled him inside. "I said thank you." She placed the chicken to rest on a clean towel in the middle of the table. "And to come inside because it is snowing." Grabbing the cups from earlier that were washed, she poured him a fresh cup of coffee and pointed to the table. "Please. You ran out so quickly this morning. Let me get you a few biscuits. I apologize, there isn't any bacon left over. I'm afraid the children were rather hungry."

"Please don't apologize. I'm surprised there were biscuits left."

She gave a little laugh. "There weren't. I made a second batch. I figured once their little bellies were full, they wouldn't eat as much."

"I need to wash my hands first," he said, glancing at Gina, who wiped her hands on a towel that was draped over the back of a chair. Once he was done, he helped himself to a biscuit from the covered basket on the table and took a seat at the table. He took a bite and closed his eyes, allowing the flaky dough to melt on his tongue. *Not even his Ma made biscuits this light!*

"I think that is the best biscuit I've ever had," he said, polishing it off in three bites before grabbing another.

Gina sat down with her coffee and pushed a jar of jelly towards him. "Try it with this. I'm not sure what kind of jelly it is."

Joe opened the jar and spread some of the dark preserves on top of his biscuit before biting in with relish. "Blackberry. Ma and my niece gathered them down by the creek." He licked the last bit of jam from his fingers and wiped his hands on his pants. "Thank you. You were right. Those were the best biscuits I've ever tasted." He leaned over and whispered to her, "Just don't tell my Ma, okay?"

Her eyes twinkled as she smiled. "I promise. Thank you for the chicken. I'll cook it all afternoon and it should be ready for dinner tonight."

"How's the boy?"

"He still has a nasty cough, but he came out to eat. I sent him back to bed."

Thick snow appeared outside the windows, falling fast, and caking the corners of the glass in frosty crystals. Joe stood in a fluid motion and went to look at the barn and the surrounding landscape. Trees were quickly disappearing under heavy blankets of white, their limbs pointing towards the ground. He could feel the cold seeping in through the edges of the window. He made a note to get a blanket to cover the glass to keep the cold out.

"I'd ride to get the doctor, but I don't think we'll be going anywhere for a bit."

"I can't afford to pay a doctor."

He returned to the table and dropped into the chair. "Doc isn't like that. He's more concerned about his patients. Folks pay him what they can afford." He gave a light laugh. "I remember when we were in town and Ma Baker comes strolling into town with a pig behind her. Walks right up to Doc's office, proud as can be. Drops off that suckling pig and heads right out of town. Doc just stood there and was like, 'What am I going to do with a suckling pig?'"

"Why would she do that?"

"She didn't have a way to pay him and he took care of her daughters."

Gina got up to refill their mugs. "What did he do with the pig?"

"Mind if I have another biscuit?" When she pushed the plate towards him, he continued. "That pig stayed in his office for a week. He trained it to go outside to... um... you know. Finally, Mr. Chapman came to town. Took that pig home to raise and butchered it for Doc in the fall."

Gina put her fingers to her chest and gasped. "That's horrible!"

"That's life out here. It wasn't a pet. Fed Doc all winter." He finished his biscuit and brushed the crumbs off his fingers. "What did you expect, moving west?"

"I don't know. We were going to live in the city. David promised me a house with glass windows and yellow curtains."

"What did your husband do?"

"He was a confectioner."

"Like a candy maker?"

Gina nodded. "He made these beautiful, boiled sugar creations. His sweets were in high demand at Christmas time."

"Why head west then?"

"I don't follow politics, but David did. There were talks of skirmishes near Ft. Sumpter, and David was afraid that soon war was going to be knocking on our door. He wanted to get us out before anything happened. So, we knew of some people heading towards Independence. We joined them and David decided we would go towards Oregon, and he would set up shop there." She splayed her hands out on the table. "Silly, isn't it? Now that I say it out loud."

Joe gently covered her hand with his own and gave it a gentle squeeze. "No. He was doing what he needed to do to protect his family. Now I don't know what all is out in Oregon apart from trees, but I'm sure they would have enjoyed a—what did you call him—a confectioner, out there."

"All I have left are his sugar molds and his recipes. We were carrying those out west."

"How did he die?"

"The doctor said it was cholera." She stared out the window, no emotion on her face. "Came from drinking dirty water." Lifting her eyes to Joe, the pain still flickered in her eyes, glossy from unshed tears. "I don't understand why he died. There were so many sick, but he died."

"I don't know, Gina." He didn't have any words of comfort for her.

She looked out the window for another minute, then stood suddenly, as if she hadn't been mourning the moment before. "I can't sit around here dilly dallying. I have this chicken to tend to."

"Where's Bethany?"

"She went to lie down; said she was tired. Honestly, I think she's happy to be warm and safe." Joe watched as Gina yanked the last of the pin feathers out with such force that she was going to remove the bird's skin.

"I'm glad she feels comfortable here."

Quartering the chicken, she placed it in a large stew pot and added water from a pitcher. Cutting a few vegetables from the root cellar, she added them to the pot before covering it and carrying to the fire. Once the pot was settled over the coals, she turned back to Joe.

"I'll make dumplings once the chicken cooks down. Will you and your brother join us for dinner?"

"I know Devin said he was hoping you'd ask."

She looked at him demurely, her eyes softening beneath dark lashes. "What about you, Joe? Are you happy I asked?" Threading her fingers through her hair, she pushed several strands behind one ear. "Would you enjoy sharing a meal with us?"

He wondered if there was another question there. He shook his head to dismiss his silly thoughts. It was a crazy notion. One put there by a little girl and then reinforced by his brother's foolishness. Gina was asking him to share a meal. *That was all.* It was simply in gratitude for allowing her family to stay at the cabin.

He wasn't going to read anything else into it.

Joe picked up the empty plate and lifted it towards her. "If dinner will be anything like these biscuits, then yes, ma'am, I most definitely am."

CHAPTER FIVE

It had been nearly a week since Gina had seen Joe and she was about to go stir crazy in the cabin. Which made no sense since she'd been stuck in a line shack with just the children and hadn't felt that way.

But that was before Joe.

Gina slid the needle through the sock, weaving it around the edges of the hole and then back around itself before pulling it tight. Once the hole was closed, she knotted the yarn before cutting it. Stretching the sock to make sure the stitching held, she added the sock to the growing pile of clothes she had repaired over the past three days.

She smiled wistfully as she recalled dinner that second night at the cabin.

He and Devin made quick work of the chicken and dumplings and made sure they stacked the inside wall with enough wood in case neither one of them could make it to the cabin during the snow. Thank goodness for their foresight, as there was at least two feet on the ground by morning. She opened the door to find a bucket of milk, partially frozen, on the porch, but the tracks leading from the barn to the house had already filled in with fresh snow.

By noon, the snow had drifted up to the door.

By evening, she couldn't even see the barn.

The snow ended the following day and Gina worked to clear the porch, using every available pot and pitcher to collect the snow. Bethany and Thomas thought it was a game. She didn't want Thomas outside, so he carried the pitchers and pots and placed them by the fire. Once the melted snow was warm enough, she filled up a galvanized washtub and bathed the children and sent them to bed.

After dumping the dirty water and refilling the tub, Gina relished her first heated bath in nearly a year. Cold baths in the river kept them clean, but there was something truly luxurious about being able to enjoy the feel of warm water against her skin. She even found a bar of lye soap and washed her hair twice before brushing it dry in front of the fire.

When she was done, she gathered up all the clothes, including any clothes she found that belonged to Joseph, and gave them a good scrub in the washtub. By the time she discarded the water, it was the color of coal. She stoked the fire and hung the items to dry in the great room, so they were dry by morning.

She enjoyed her bath so much; she did it again that very next evening, this time washing the bed sheets afterwards.

Waste not, want not, her mother taught her.

I wonder what he's doing? she thought as she picked up another sock and formed it around her fist. Taking the needle, she inserted it at the end of the hole and started weaving the thread back and forth, humming lightly as she worked. She missed doing domestic chores.

What would it be like if Joe were her husband?
He'd be out hunting, and she'd be here in the house
with their children, waiting for him to return. The
house would be clean as a pin. Hot coffee and fresh
biscuits would always be ready for when he came
back with a fresh kill for dinner.

She'd greet him with a kiss and fuss over the
bounty he provided for them. She'd prepare a feast
fit for a king, while he rested from his long hunt
until time for supper. After the meal, Bethany
would clean up and Joe would read from the Bible
before bedtime.

What a wonderful vision. If it could only be
true.

She imagined Joe would be an excellent
provider.

Looking around the house, she couldn't help
but appreciate the hard work that went into
building such a sturdy home. It was a lovely cabin,
made from hand sawed lumber, and well insulated.
Not a draft penetrated the mud and moss chinking.

The cabin was one large room with the doors
on either side of the main room. There was only

sparse furniture adorning the interior. A large table took up a portion of the room, along with a dry sink and a workbench. The carpenter had built two cupboards into the corners, and between them was the enormous fireplace. Gina wondered if Joe brought the stones from the river to create such a magnificent hearth.

Life here was different than the hustle of Charleston. Everyone was so busy rushing back and forth. There were shops on every corner, parties almost every evening, barely a moment to rest. David had promised her a different life out west, but he still wanted to move to what he imagined would be a city.

What would be the difference between a city on the east coast versus a city on the west coast? Gina thought it was just a location. *Aren't all cities just the same?* A melting pot of people that barely know each other? Never slowing down, always racing from one thing to the next?

And with the war looming on the horizon, Gina was glad to be as far away from the city as possible.

David would never be happy in a place like Flat River. He always said he didn't like small town life. And he didn't handle the hardships of the trail well. Yes, he thought it was an adventure at first, but the man who was used to suits and having everything right at his fingertips wasn't prepared for how desolate life would be, or how far apart it was between trail stations.

Now that she wasn't trying to just survive, Gina could find herself delighted in a small cabin in the middle of the woods. *Especially if she had a husband like Joe.*

She wondered how long would be appropriate before she considered marrying again. She knew several widows in Charleston who claimed they would never marry. Those were also rich widows who didn't need to rely on anyone for their next meal or shelter.

On the wagon train, there was one woman whose husband died. She turned around and married the man's brother the very next day! Gina couldn't imagine that. But it allowed the woman to remain on the wagon train and continue west with her family.

Picking up another sock, she thought about the two Moore brothers and mentally checked off the positive attributes she had picked up in her short time knowing them.

Both were incredibly handsome.

And kind.

They were well-mannered.

Generous.

Honorable.

She continued until she had finished the sock and added it to the basket before retrieving another. Giving a giggle, she wondered how many socks one man could have with so many holes?

If Joseph had at least a dozen, she wondered how many Devin might have?

So far, she had washed two pairs of pants and several shirts, along with the many socks. There wasn't one item that didn't need cleaning or mending.

Yes, these men needed wives.

Perhaps it might be worth a conversation with one of them. That way, she wouldn't have to worry about having to move again.

If Joe wasn't interested in getting married, perhaps Devin might be. She didn't recall seeing many women in town when she was there, although she wasn't looking. Yes, it would be worth a conversation.

Knotting off the yarn on the final sock, she heard boots pounding against the porch, followed by three sharp knocks.

"Gina?"

Her heart soared as Joe's voice carried through the thick wood. Dropping the sock in the basket, she raced to the door to open it. Smiling, she spied Joe, his arms full of wood and four plump, freshly cleaned rabbits dangling from his hand. He took a step forward, but stopped abruptly, eyes opening wide as they appreciatively swept over her.

She cleared her throat, pretending not to be affected by his gaze.

"Come in. You're letting all the heat out," she gently scolded, standing back to let him in.

"You look—"

"Clean?"

He leaned his head back and laughed. "Beautiful. Take these," he offered, handing her the rabbits. "I'll see how much wood you have left, and I wanted to let you know that it is clear enough that we can go to town tomorrow."

"Oh good! I was hoping I might be able to get a few things..." she looked around the room to make sure the children weren't within earshot, "for Christmas for the children."

Walking by, he placed a kiss on her cheek and proceeded to the fireplace to add the sticks to the dwindling pile.

Gina quickly shut the door, then raised her hand to her cheek, hoping to keep the warmth of his kiss before it disappeared. *He kissed her!*

That was it. Forget Devin.

She was going to marry Joe.

"Would you like a cup of coffee?"

He pulled off his gloves and placed them on the table, unwrapping the scarf from around his neck. "I'd love a cup if you have any handy."

"I can make a fresh pot. Give me a few minutes." Hanging the rabbits on the back of the chair, she grabbed the coffeepot and the can of coffee.

"I'm surprised you don't have a pot already

brewing."

"I've been careful about your supplies. I have no way to pay you back and I heard what you said about them needing to last you until spring."

"Hmm." He clasped his hands together and rubbed them.

"What do you need to get for the children?"

"Excuse me?"

"You said you wanted to get some items for the children."

"Oh! I made them mittens, but I would like to get them a few sweets. Maybe an apple. I'd like to bake them some cakes, but I didn't want to use any extra supplies."

"Make a list of whatever you need. I can replace enough for a few cakes and pies. There is a dinner at the Chapmans on Christmas Eve. Ma normally contributes for Devin and me. I don't know if you would like to make something, but I'd sure appreciate it if you would."

"I'd like that. Let me think about what I could make. Maybe a dried fruit cake or a buttermilk pie. Those won't take much work."

"How's Thomas?"

"Much better. He still has a bit of a cough." Adding water to the pot, she walked it over to the fire. "They are in the room reading. Would you like to see them?"

Joe smiled. "I would."

Before Gina could call them, the door to the bedroom clattered open and the two children raced out.

"Joe!" Bethany called. "I thought I heard you." She raced into his outstretched arms. Thomas gave a quick cough as Joe pulled him into a quick embrace. "We've missed you. It has been so boring."

Joe laughed, and he released the children. "Well, I'm sure that you kept yourself busy." He looked around the house. "I don't think I've ever seen this room look so clean before. Did you help your Ma?"

"Well, Tommy didn't."

"Did too," Thomas said, knocking his sister with an elbow. "I carried the snow to the fire to melt."

Gina kissed the top of his head. "Yes, you did. That was an important job."

"What's all this?" Joe leaned over and picked up a sock from the basket on the floor.

Bethany danced around the room. "Ma fixed your clothes."

Joe's eyes snapped to Gina. "Is that true?"

Gina nodded, clasping her hands in front of her. "Are you angry?"

"Not angry. Just surprised." He placed the sock back in the basket and picked up a shirt. "I tore this on a branch. Looks as good as new." Holding it close to his nose, he sniffed the fabric. "Smells good too. You did laundry?"

"I wanted to pay you back. You were so kind to allow us to stay here."

A scowl formed over his handsome features, and a warning voice whispered in her head. *Perhaps she overstepped her bounds.*

"You didn't have to do anything," he growled. "I wasn't expecting payment of any kind for you to stay here."

Gina held her hands tighter to stop them from

shaking. "I know, but I wanted to. Besides, you deserve to wear socks that don't have holes in them. I would do the same for Devin."

His gaze traveled over her face and searched her eyes as if looking for something, and his scowl deepened. "Devin can fix his own clothes, and Ma does his laundry. You don't need to be doing a thing for Devin."

Gina grasped the back of the chair and fingered the string holding the rabbits. "You are grown men and your mother does your laundry?"

"Why not? It's woman's work."

She turned to face him, her temper flaring. "So is darning and fixing rips. Cooking and cleaning and keeping house. It appears, however, Mr. Moore, that none of those things had been happening here for a long time. Why there was so much soot in here, I could have used it to teach the children how to write their names."

Crossing his arms over his chest, he replied sharply, "Just what are you saying, *Mrs. Graham*?"

The way he said her name infuriated and delighted her.

"You need a wife." She poked her finger in his

75

chest.

"I do not need…"

"Joe?" Thomas tugged on Joe's sleeve. When the man didn't respond, he tugged harder. "Joe?"

Joe looked down, his expression instantly softening as he looked at the young boy. "What is it?"

"If you need a wife, does this mean you are going marry Ma and be our Pa?"

Joe opened his mouth and quickly closed it.

Before he could answer, Gina responded, "No! That's all Tommy. Don't bother Joe with such silliness. Go wash up for supper. Are you staying?"

"I could have answered for myself, I'll have you know."

"I'm sure you can." Putting a hand on her hip, she wrinkled her nose. "So, Mr. Moore, are you staying or not?"

"I'd be delighted to stay." He punctuated each word and sat down at the table.

"Bethany, grab the stew pot and let's get these rabbits started."

"You certainly act like you're married,"

Bethany mumbled as she did what her mother asked.

As Gina picked up the rabbit to cut it into smaller pieces, she noticed Joe was smiling. He must have heard what Bethany said as well. Clearing his throat, he pretended to glower at her as she turned away. A large smile broke from her lips as she was wrapped in a cocoon of domestic bliss.

CHAPTER SIX

Gina wrapped her two shawls around her shoulders and a third one over her ears. She looked as bulky as the snowman Bethany made in the barnyard, but at least she would be warm on the way to town.

Tomorrow was Christmas Eve, and the snow had melted enough that Joe wanted to make a trip to town. He insisted Gina ride with him, and Devin would watch the children while they were away.

It was a fortuitous opportunity, as she wanted to go to town, if only to get a few items for the children for Christmas. She had five cents that she could spare to get some peppermint candy and maybe an apple, if the store had any. If there was any money when she was done, she would purchase a bar of scented soap. It was an extravagance, but she wanted something that didn't smell like ashes and animal fat.

She had talked to Joe and Devin about their Christmas plans and what a feast they were going to have on Christmas Day! Gina had already baked small spice cakes dotted with some dried fruit she found and put them in the larder to cool. Tomorrow, she would decorate them with a sugar icing that would balance the ginger and cinnamon flavors.

Bethany helped Gina bake cookies to take to the Chapman's, and she found enough ingredients to make two vinegar pies. She wrapped up one to take to their hostess tomorrow and the other they would enjoy with their Christmas meal.

Devin provided a ham that needed to be soaked to remove most of the salt-cure, along with some sweet potatoes and a jar of pickles. When they got back from the Christmas Eve celebration, Gina would make bread and allow it to rise overnight before baking it in the morning.

Christmas was a fancier affair in Charleston, with decadent parties, champagne, and an overabundance of food. So much so that a lot of the food would go to waste. It excited Gina for the opportunity to experience a true prairie Christmas with her children.

She walked to the window to look at the barnyard. Joe was just exiting the barn and walking his horse towards the house. Joe had already saddled Chestnut, and two large saddlebags bounced on his flanks. He wore the same coat as the day she first saw him. *Oh my, he is handsome,* she thought, as she watched him approach.

"You be good, you hear?" she said to the children, leaning down to give them each a quick kiss.

Tommy coughed into his arm and pulled the blanket tighter around him. "When are you coming back?"

"It shouldn't be more than a few hours." She leaned down to look the little boy in the eye. "Why don't you lie down and take a nap? I'll probably be back by the time you wake up."

Tommy nodded, and lifting the edge of the

blanket, he wandered back towards the back room.

"Is there anything you want me to do while you are gone, Mama?" Bethany asked.

"Just make sure the fire doesn't go out, but don't build it up too much. We don't want to burn the cabin down."

"Can I bake a cake?"

"No, honey. I won't be here to watch you. Wait until I get back. But if you want to start the bread for tomorrow, you can do that. We can bake it later tonight." Gina pulled her daughter tight and gave her a hug.

"I can't believe Christmas will be here in two days."

"I know, sweetheart. It will be a small Christmas, but we have much to be thankful for."

"Do you like Joe?"

Gina released her daughter and stepped back. "What kind of question is that?"

"I was just wondering."

"I do like him. I'm very grateful that he has given us a home and food in our bellies. He is a wonderful friend."

"Do you want to kiss him?"

"Bethany! Where do you get such foolish notions, child? No, I do not want to kiss him."

It was a lie. Gina wanted to kiss Joe very much.

"What do you…"

The sound of Joe knocking interrupted Bethany's question, and Gina was very grateful.

"Love you. Watch after your brother and I'll be back as quickly as possible. And mind Mr. Moore." Gina opened the door and Joe looked at her, a frown appearing as his eyes took in her appearance.

"Are you going to town like that?" he asked, pushing his way inside.

Gina looked down and twirled from left to right. "This is all I have."

"You'll freeze before we get halfway there."

"What do you want me to do?"

"I don't have an extra coat, but I have some heavy shirts. Maybe if you put on two of those and then put on the shawls and a blanket. Let me grab them. Is Tommy asleep?"

"Not yet. He just went to lie down."

Joe's boots thudded across the wooden floor. "Hi, sweetie," he said, ruffing Bethany's hair. "Devin will be over shortly." Gina followed him to the bedroom. "Hey buddy. How are you feeling?"

Tommy gave a little cough. "Better. Just tired."

"Well, you rest up. I just need to get something out of here. That OK with you?" When Tommy nodded, Joe went to the wardrobe in the corner and pulled out two heavy wool shirts, handing them to Gina. "Here. Put these over your dress. They should keep you warm. Grab an extra blanket for your legs. We'll look for a coat at the store."

"Joe, I can't…"

"Gina, just get dressed, and let's go. I want to get back before dark."

She nodded and began removing her threadbare wraps, embarrassed that she didn't have proper clothes. Joe took one last look at her and left the room. She heard Devin's voice in the main room talking to Joe.

Her stomach pitted into tight knots as their voices lowered to a whisper. Were they talking about her? Did Joe tell his brother about the state of her clothing?

Shame flushed her cheeks.

"Mama?" Tommy said, reaching out to grab her arm. "Do you have a fever?"

"What?" She turned to her son, ignoring the sounds of laughter coming from the living room. "No, honey, why?"

"Because you are all red."

Quickly buttoning up the shirt, she pressed her hands to her cheeks to cool the fiery flames. *Why were children so observant?* "I am just putting on such warm clothing while I'm still inside." Leaning over to brush Tommy's hair away from his bright eyes, she pressed a kiss against his forehead. "You go to sleep. I'll be home soon."

Tommy rolled over, taking the covers with him, and Gina heard his light snores before she reached the bedroom door.

"Is he asleep?" Devin asked, scraping a wooden chair across the floor before lowering his tall frame onto it.

"He is. He'll be asleep for a bit." Gina tugged on her worn gloves. "Thank you for watching the children."

"My pleasure. I gave Joe a list of things to pick up for me."

"Remember, I don't have a wagon," Joe said, picking up the blanket and placing his hand on Gina's back.

"You'll figure out a way, brother." Turning to Bethany, he asked, "So, are you going to teach me how to bake?"

"Ma said I had to have an adult here."

Devin pounded his chest. "What do I look like?"

"An overgrown child. Come on, Gina. We'll be back soon. You be good."

"We will, Joe," Bethany called.

"I was talking to Devin."

Gina laughed. "Don't burn down your brother's home."

She walked outside and the bitter air filled her lungs. Joe was right. She wouldn't make it to town before the cold overcame her. Wrapping the blanket around her like a cape, she pulled the edges together and held them tight against her chest and walked to the edge of the porch.

"Just wait there," Joe directed, untying his horse from the railing in front of the house.

"What do you want me to do?"

He moved Chestnut backwards and mounted him in one smooth motion before walking the animal in front of Gina. The horse was too tall, and Gina didn't know how she could climb behind Joe, let alone hold on to the blanket for the long ride to town.

He reached his arm down. "Let go of your blanket and I'll lift you up."

"How will I get the blanket back around me?"

"You won't." Gina lifted her eyebrow, not sure why he asked her to bring a cover. "Trust me. Please."

Gina pulled her blanket-cape from around her shoulders with a swish and draped the coverlet over one arm. Using her free hand, she reached out to Joe, fully prepared to take her place at the back of the horse.

She felt herself being lifted in the air and found herself instead on the front of the saddle, the wooden saddle horn sticking in the back of her thigh. She couldn't ride to town like that. *I'll have bruises where I shouldn't have bruises*, she thought.

"This is very uncomfortable." Gina twisted slightly, trying to get the horn out of her thigh. Joe sniggered. "And not funny."

"Give me the blanket." Taking the blanket, he put it over his lap, between him and Gina. "I'm going to lift you slightly. You'll need to adjust your skirt and hook your leg over the horn, like you are riding sidesaddle."

"What do I do with the other one?"

The horse, feeling her trepidation, moved forward. Gina lurched and grabbed onto Joe's arm.

"Just let it hang."

"What if I fall off?" she asked, tightening her grip on his arm.

His breath was hot against her ear. "I won't let you fall. I promise," he murmured.

Her flesh came alive with small tingles racing over her skin. If he did that again, she wouldn't need the blanket at all to keep her warm. Swallowing hard, she gave a brief nod. "One. Two. Three."

He lifted her up, and she pulled her skirt so the fabric wasn't tight against her legs, and she could easily move over the saddle horn. She was now trapped in his embrace, but leaning forward as the blanket pressed against her back.

Suddenly the blanket was gone, and everything went dark, before her vision appeared once more. Joe draped the blanket over her front and pulled her tight against his chest.

"Oh!" she cried.

"Lean back. It will be easier to ride that way." Gina hesitated. "I will not take advantage of you, Gina, if that is what you are worried about."

That is exactly what she was worried about. And maybe that is exactly what she wanted.

Relaxing her shoulders, she allowed herself to lean backwards into his warm embrace. He held the reins with one hand and moved his arm over the blanket. Then repeated it until both hands were outside the blanket and he could tuck the fabric around her shoulders.

She had never been so warm in her life. It was lovely.

Giving a little sigh, she allowed herself to relax

and enjoy the feel of Joe's arms around her.

Joe clicked his tongue and gently pulled on the reins. The horse started walking in a circle away from the house and towards the tree line. As they were turning, Gina spied a quick movement from the window and saw Devin and Bethany with their noses pressed against the glass. Bethany gave a little wave as Devin lifted his head and laughed.

CHAPTER SEVEN

It was a good thing Chestnut knew the way to town. Joe could barely concentrate on anything, but the woman nestled in his arms. She fit perfectly, as if God made her just for him. How he wished that was the case. But Gina had been married before and had birthed two beautiful children.

He wondered, if they were to get married, what their children might look like.

Would they have hair the color of rich whiskey?

Or would it be drab like his?

Would they be petite, like her?

Or burly, like the rest of the Moore family?

"I can smell smoke," Gina said, adjusting herself in the saddle. "And my leg has fallen asleep."

Joe relaxed his arms around her, and he felt the sudden shift in temperature. "Is that better?"

"I just need to move a little to the left."

Joe held his arms in a circle so he would catch her if she fell. She shifted, and Joe felt every nerve in his body snap to attention. The scarf covering her hair fell, and those whiskey-colored locks he was just daydreaming about brushed his nose. He tightened his thighs next to her, and she froze.

"Are you done?" he asked. She nodded, her back straight, as she reached one hand from beneath the blanket to cover her hair again. Joe bit his lower lip, but it was no use. A groan escaped, as if he were a man being tortured. "Could you not?"

Gina whipped her head around, her hand catching him in the nose. "What? Oh my goodness, Joe! I am so sorry."

Thankful for the reprieve, Joe lifted a gloved hand to his nose. His eyes smarted and he could feel tears forming behind the stars, blocking his vision. "Just turn around and sit still."

He blinked rapidly until his vision cleared and shook his head, trying to release some of the pain from the impact.

"I didn't mean to hit you," she mumbled.

"Hold the reins." He placed them in her blanket covered hand. When he felt her fingers gripping them tightly through the fabric, he released the leather and lifted her scarf back over her head. "I know you didn't." He wrapped the end of the scarf several times around her neck before tucking it underneath itself. "Better?"

When Gina nodded, he took the reins back, but continued to keep his arm loose. His other hand he left on his leg, not risking wrapping it back around her. He didn't want to get used to having her in his arms.

"How much longer do you think?"

"We aren't even to the edge of the property yet. Once we are there, then it will be another thirty or forty minutes."

"Why so long?"

"Well, the snow hasn't melted in the forest. Once we get past the cabin where you were staying at, and then past the woods and the creek, the sun should have melted everything on the prairie. Chestnut should be able to go a little faster."

"I'm sorry I took your traps. I didn't know they were yours. We were just so hungry."

Joe blew the ends of the scarf from his face. "I know you were. I would have done the same if it meant feeding my family."

"Joe?"

"Yes, Gina?"

"Can you put your arms back around me? I was warmer that way."

Joe gave a little smile, grateful that Gina couldn't see him. Truthfully, he was warmer, too. "Are you trying to take advantage of me?" he teased.

"Only if it keeps me warm on the ride to town."

Laughing out loud, he lifted his hand from his thigh and brought it around to grasp the reins. "Better?"

"Much." She leaned back into his arms again.

"So, tell me about your life before your trip out here."

"What do you want to know?"

"Where are you from? How did you meet your husband? You seem young to have two children."

"A woman never reveals her age."

"Okay. I'm going to say that you are thirty-three. You married your husband to get away from some poor sop that your parents were planning on having you marry, and you were running away west to live happily ever after."

Gina huffed. "I am not thirty-three."

"Ah! But you don't deny the rest."

"Actually, David was the man my parents arranged for me to marry."

Joe snorted. "Really?"

"Yes. They do things differently in Charleston."

"That's where you said you were from?"

Gina nodded and pulled the blanket tighter around her as if she were protecting herself from memories. "I'm twenty-four. Bethany is eight.

Thomas is five. You can do the math."

"You were…" Joe went silent for a moment. "You were just a child."

"It was very common to be married at sixteen. But that is the way things were. It was a financial match. To keep the money in the family, so to speak. But then David decided he wanted to be a confectioner. He was actually very good at it. My family wasn't happy. They thought he was going to be a solicitor or a politician. It was quite a scandal when he opened his shop, but David appeared to be thrilled, and his candy was the attraction of all the upper echelon parties."

"What made you leave Charleston?"

"There's a war coming. South Carolina finally seceded from the Union and that's all the men talked about. War. War. War. Not today, maybe not tomorrow, but soon. David didn't want us to be there when the war broke out. So, we packed up and moved. I didn't want to go, but what was I supposed to do? He was my husband."

"He wanted to keep you safe. I can't fault him for that."

"But he didn't. I hated everything about this

trip." Joe thought he heard her sniffle. "I had to learn to milk a cow and cook outdoors."

"That's why you are good at cooking on the hearth, then."

Gina gave a harsh laugh. "I burned two skirts on the trip. I learned quickly after that." She wiped her tears on the edge of the blanket. "You must think I do nothing but cry."

Pulling her tighter into his embrace, Joe pressed his cheek against her head. "I think you've been through some hard times, and you deserve to cry a little."

"The women on the wagon train thought I was weak. I guess I was. I went from being coddled to the harsh realities of the world."

"Weren't you the least bit excited about going out west? Wasn't there one thing that made it worthwhile?"

"Despite being alone and trying to survive, I have to say I enjoyed our days in the cabin by the creek." She turned to glance over her shoulder at Joe. "At least until it turned cold. But the summer and fall were pleasant enough."

"I bet you learned plenty of new skills living on

your own."

"I did. It was a godsend when I found those traps. I had never butchered a rabbit before. My first one wasn't pretty."

"Maybe I can teach you how to do it properly."

"I hope I won't ever have to do it again."

"I can understand that, too."

"How can you live out here, Joe? It is so wild."

"Wild but beautiful. I can't imagine being anywhere else. My family is here."

"My family is still in Charleston. I can't help but worry about them."

"Maybe you and the children will find a new family."

"Hmmm. Tell me about your family."

"We immigrated to New York from Ireland. There was a famine, and food was in short supply, so people were leaving on these big ships destined for America. I was eight. Devin was nine. Dorie was thirteen and Liam was ten. Liam got sick on the voyage over and never recovered."

"I am so sorry, Joe."

"That's probably why I know what it is like to

be starving and to lose someone you love."

"How did you get from New York to here?"

"Conditions in the city were harsh and Pa couldn't find work. Dev and I were too young. He didn't want to see Ma and Dorie worked to death; and he heard about the wagon train headed west. He took what money he had left and got a wagon and some horses, and we went to Independence, where we joined a group headed to the Pacific coast. We took a detour to this little town and Pa liked it so much that we stayed. Made a claim and have built an enjoyable life. Dorie got married and had two kids. She and her husband live in the same clearing as Ma and Pa."

"It doesn't seem like there is much out here."

"There isn't, but the people are the nicest you'll ever meet, and they come together when needed. I can't imagine a more perfect place on earth to live."

"I can see why. Your house is beautiful and the place where you live is like a little corner of Heaven."

A warmth filled Joe's chest. He was proud of the homes he and Devin had built. Even though they didn't have much, the entire family was rich in those things that mattered.

"Do you like the cabin?"

"I do. I never thought I'd be happy outside the city, but if I was to be happy anywhere, I'm sure it would be there."

"I'm glad. Gina, there was something I wanted to ask you."

Gina turned slightly in the saddle. "Yes, Joe?"

The unexpected sound of rustling near the bushes distracted Joe, followed by the quiet gaggle from a flock of wild turkeys. Stopping the horse, Joe put a finger to his lips and handed Gina the reins. He pulled the rifle from its scabbard and slid off the horse, wincing as the snow crunched beneath his boots.

Gina looked at him, fear glittering in her eyes. He gave her a little wave and moved as silently as he could towards the line of bushes. Peering over them, he raised the rifle to his shoulder and fired once, twice, as half a dozen birds took flight for the shelter of the trees.

"Got'um!" Joe yelled as he pushed through the bushes.

"Got what?"

Joe walked around the bushes and held up two plump birds by their legs. "Christmas Dinner!"

Gina clapped her hands. "How wonderful."

Joe handed the birds to Gina. "Hold these."

Gina stopped clapping and wrinkled her nose. "I don't think so."

"Why not?"

"They are … well, you know. Dead," she whispered loudly.

"You didn't have a problem a few minutes ago talking about butchering a rabbit."

"That was different. I didn't know it when it was alive."

"Fine. Hold my rifle. I need to get a bag." Handing the rifle to Gina, he rummaged in the saddle bag until he found two flour sacks to place the birds in. "Tie these to the saddle horn while I quickly wipe my rifle and wash my hands."

She handed Joe back his rifle and took one bag. "But my leg is on the saddle horn."

"Then you'll just have to lift your leg, so they swing to the other side." Sliding the rifle in the scabbard, Joe left Gina and headed down to the edge of the creek to wash his hands. By the time he returned, she was off the horse and the turkey bags were draped over the saddle horn.

"I couldn't balance myself, so I thought it would be easier to just slide off and fix it."

"Let's get you back up then."

Gina moved closer to him. "Not yet."

Joe pushed his hat back so he could see her. She had pulled the blanket up around her head and was holding it beneath her chin. She looked so childlike; Joe couldn't help but grin. "Why not?"

"You said you wanted to ask me a question."

Joe moved closer. He did. So many questions swirled through his mind. Cupping her face, he lifted it up so he could look into those golden eyes. "You are breathtaking, Gina. You've taken my breath away. I've wanted to kiss you for days. May I? May I kiss you?"

Her lips parted and a small puff of breath appeared in the cold air. "I want that too, Joe."

It was all the invitation he needed to lean down and kiss the tip of her nose. "Your nose is cold," he murmured. Then he kissed her eyelids. "So are your eyes." He moved to her forehead and each cheek before claiming her lips with a soft kiss. She didn't resist succumbing to the sweetness of his kiss.

He felt her knees weaken, so he pulled her closer to him, deepening the kiss.

What this woman did to him!

She released the blanket, as he felt it fall over the arms that were holding her. Her fingers shyly reached out and curled around his upper arms.

Joe knew then that he never wanted to let her go. He wanted to spend the rest of his life protecting, providing for, *and kissing* her.

When he finally broke the kiss, he could barely breathe. Gina's eyes were still closed, so he gently brushed his lips against hers once more, then rubbed his nose against hers.

"Are you warmer?"

"I am," she cooed, opening her eyes halfway. She gave him a smile that would have melted the ice all the way to the Rockies.

"Let's get to town. We need to see the Doc and

pick up some supplies."

Joe hoisted himself on top of Chestnut and reached down to hoist Gina in front of him. This time, he didn't even pretend to maintain an air of decorum. He wrapped the blanket around her and pulled her tight against his chest, pressing his cheek against her hair.

Yes, he could get very used to having her in his arms. In fact, once they were done with town, Joe decided he was going to ask her to marry him on the way home.

CHAPTER EIGHT

Joe pushed open the door to the mercantile and guided Gina inside, his hand resting on the small of her back.

"I thought we were going to see the Marshal," she said. Her voice had a slight tremor to it, but Joe ignored it. There wasn't anything for her to fear. He would make sure of it.

"He's normally in here. There's a potbelly stove and plenty of coffee." The inside of the store was warm compared to the bitter cold outside. Joe shut the door behind him and moved towards the iron stove. "Why don't you sit here for a few minutes," he said, "and get yourself warm. I'm just going to give my list to Dillon and then I need to talk to the doctor about Tommy."

Gina looked worried as she gazed around the small store.

Flat River was still a tiny town, so the shop wasn't large, but it carried enough supplies for the hundred-or-so residents who called it home. There weren't many supplies on the shelves as the last wagon with supplies came through in September, but there was always coffee on and friendly conversation to be had.

Conversation was Joe's aim. He needed information and then he had a decision to make.

He patted Gina on the shoulder and headed to the counter to speak with Dillon Arden, who owned the mercantile.

"Joe!" Dillon said, looking up from his ledger. "What brings you in today? I wasn't expecting to see you until spring."

Joe pulled out a piece of paper and put it on the counter. "Are you going to the Chapmans tomorrow?"

"We are. Rose is upstairs, making her pies as

we speak." Picking up the paper, Dillon opened it and scanned the list, his eyes opening wide. "What's this about?"

"I was wondering if you might bring those items with you? I'll pay delivery, of course. I can pick them up there. Saves me having to come back to town. I only have my horse with me today."

"I'm not sure if I have everything in stock. I thought you had all your supplies for winter."

Joe glanced over his shoulder at Gina, who was holding her hands out to the fire. "Things changed." Turning back to the shopkeeper Joe said, "I also need a woman's coat, if you have one and a sturdy pair of boots."

"Is that for her?" Dillon pointed to Gina with the paper. Joe nodded. "Why do I think I've seen her before?"

"She was here this summer with the wagon train. Her husband died. She's staying at my place through the winter."

"Your Ma knows?"

"Not yet." Joe lifted his finger before Dillon could say anything. "Mrs. Graham is staying at my house. I'm staying with Devin."

Dillon flexed his mouth in a silent *oh* and placed the paper down on the counter. "Whatever you say, Joe."

"I also would like to pick up a few other things. I need some fabric. Enough for a few dresses, a pair of pants for a small boy, about five years old, and a couple of shirts."

"That's Rose's department. Rose!" A few moments later, a petite woman with a round face appeared from behind a curtain hiding a wooden staircase.

"What is it?" she asked, walking over to the counter as she wiped flour from her hands.

"Joe needs a few things, and I thought you might help him."

"Alright." Glancing at Gina, she turned to Joe and smiled. "Are these for you?"

"No, ma'am."

"Come on over here and tell me what you need."

When Joe explained what he was looking for, Rose nodded and moved over to sit next to Gina by the stove. He watched as Gina listened to Rose speak, then her eyes snapped to Joe, and she shook her head.

Joe nodded his approval.

"I can't," she mouthed to him.

"You can," he mouthed back. Turning to Dillon, he patted the counter. "Whatever she needs. Take it from my credit. Can you also give me a full sack of peppermint sticks, that doll over there, that wooden horse and one of those bonnets? I'll take the peppermint sticks home. Can you wrap the rest up and bring on Christmas Eve?"

Dillon scribbled in his ledger. "Anything else?"

Joe glanced around the store. Spying a display near the window, he grinned. "Yeah. I'll take those yellow curtains."

Dillon wrote the note in the ledger and then scratched his chin. "You fixin' to marry this woman?"

"Why are you askin'?"

The shopkeeper shook his shoulders. "Just seems to me you are buying enough supplies to get a family through winter; plus outfitting this woman and her two children. Plus, setting up housekeeping."

"Maybe I am, Dillon. I just haven't asked her yet."

"Well, you know the preacher will be at Weston's on Christmas Eve. I think there are three other couples getting married."

Joe thought for a moment. "Do you know if there are any pre-made dresses available?" Joe didn't know anything about dresses, but he had seen several that were already made once or twice in the shop.

"I think Rose might have a few."

"Have her pick something out, but wrap that up and we'll take it with us when we leave. I need to run over to see Doc." He walked over to the counter where Rose had several bolts of fabric laid out in front of Gina. Joe placed his hand gently on Gina's shoulder. "I am going to walk across the street, but I'll be right back."

"Joe, I can't let you spend your hard-earned money on me or the children."

"It's my hard-earned money. I can spend it as I please." He kissed Gina gently on her hair. "I'll be right back." As he walked away, he pointed to

Rose. "Don't let her give you any grief, you hear me?"

"I hear you, Joe!" Rose called. "Now, I think with your coloring this burgundy fabric would look…"

Their voices faded as Joe ventured out into the cold once more. Flipping up the collar of his shirt against the cold, he made his way over to Doc Mueller's office. There was a small two-seater buggy tied to the hitching post outside. Joe hoped the Doc wasn't busy with a patient. As he walked in, Joe spied Mrs. Chapman and her youngest daughter talking to the physician.

"Mrs. Chapman. Doc." Joe said, entering the office. "Good afternoon, Alice. I hope you aren't ill."

Alice was a pretty girl, approximately six years old. She had her mother's gigantic eyes and her father's golden-brown hair. She shook her head. "No. Mari and Penny are sick."

Marianne and Penelope were the Chapman's ten-year-old twins, and the second set in their large family. The first set of twins, Owen and Oliver, were born when the wagon train rolled into Flat

110

River in 1840. Then Ingrid Chapman gave birth to three additional strapping boys. Finally, all the girls were born. Joe remembered when each child was born as babies were a big celebration in Flat River.

"I'm sorry to hear that." Glancing to Ingrid, he said, "I hope that doesn't mess up your plans for Christmas Eve."

"Of course not," she said, digging in her reticule. "It's just a cough. Marianne has it, but Penelope, being the dramatic one, must exaggerate and follow suit. You would think that she has the plague or something." Pulling out a coin, she smiled. "There it is! Not to worry, Joe. No one has a fever."

Doc held out a dark bottle to Mrs. Chapman. "That will be five cents. You tell those girls of yours I hope they feel better in time for Santa."

Tucking the bottle into her bag, she patted Alice on the back. "We need to get going. I ran out of cinnamon, so I must run to the mercantile and get back home."

Joe was standing in front of the door, but he didn't move aside. "Before you leave, I was wondering—"

Ingrid stopped and looked at him, blinking a few times. "Yes?"

"I have three guests staying at my house."

"Well, bring them. The more the merrier."

"Thank you. I just wanted to let you know they had been living in the shack along the creek bed."

"Orrin's cabin?" Joe nodded. "Why that isn't fit for a man or a beast. I told Weston we needed to tear it down. I thought it would be a den of rattlesnakes by now. How did they survive?"

"They were in terrible shape. Starving, their clothes are threadbare. The wagon train just left them behind. I don't think they would have made it through winter. Anyway, I wanted to let you know in case you found the cabin disturbed."

"Well thank you, Joe. If I had known, we would have made sure they were taken care of." Joe smiled. The Chapmans would have looked after the young family, he knew that. "You said they are living with you now?"

"Yes ma'am. They are staying in my cabin. I'm staying with Devin."

Ingrid tugged on her glove. "It's about time you and your brother get married. Maybe one of you should marry the poor woman."

Doc snorted in the background. Joe narrowed his eyes and looked at the good doctor, who had the decency to turn away and fiddle with the bottles in his cabinet.

"That's up to her, ma'am, being a widow and all."

"Hmm." Ingrid patted his arm. "Well, it is the season of miracles. Now get out of my way, so I can get back home. I expect to see you and this family tomorrow night."

"Yes, ma'am," Joe said, smiling as he opened the door. "Bye Alice."

"Bye, Mr. Moore!"

As he closed the door, he turned to look at the doctor, who was grinning. "What?" Joe asked.

"She's already married you off."

"No, she hasn't."

"You don't know Ingrid. She's responsible for more marriages in this town than anyone."

"There aren't enough people in this town."

"Yes, but the ones that have gotten married, she's brought them together."

"I didn't come to talk about getting married. I came to see the Marshal."

"He's gone. Anything I can help you with?"

"I was going to talk to him about what would happen with the family."

"What do you mean?"

"Like what would happen to them… you know."

Doc looked at Joe for a moment and then he nodded. "Ah. I understand. You mean what would happen once the snow melts?"

"Exactly."

"Well, the choices are limited for unmarried women out here. Most must go work at a brothel, but that isn't any place for children. If they have enough money, they might return home, or go live with relatives. Or they get married."

"That's what Devin said, too."

"Unfortunately, there's no getting around it. Women don't own property."

"Remember the wagon train that came this

summer?"

"Let me think. Yeah, there was one where a bunch of people ended up with cholera from drinking dirty water."

"That would be the one. This family was the one whose husband and father died on that trip."

"Oh land. I remember that. There wasn't anything I could do. He died rather quickly."

"They left her, Doc. Took all her supplies and left her with a lame mare, some personal items and a broken-down wagon."

Doc shook his head. "I told you, son, women don't own property. Unless she was prepared to fight, I'm not surprised that they took everything. What I am surprised about is that they survived this long alone out there in that drafty cabin."

"About that. I need something because the boy has a horrible rattle in his chest."

"Fever?"

"That broke. Just the rattle when he speaks or coughs."

"Did you give him an onion poultice?"

"Yeah. Made the house smell terrible.

115

Loosened up his chest, but then the coughing worsened."

"Sounds like the Winter Fever. Let me make something up for you to give him. Want a cup of coffee while you wait?"

"No, thanks. I need to get back to the mercantile. I left Gina over there."

"Gina?"

"I mean Mrs. Graham."

Doc grinned as he turned back to his potions. "Hmmm. You don't know how bad you got it, Joe."

It didn't take long before Joe had the bottle tucked inside the pocket of his coat and he was jogging back toward the store. The temperature had dropped, and he wanted to get home as quickly as possible before Tommy's medicine froze.

Maybe he did have it bad.

He thought about the feel of Gina in his arms.

He recalled how enjoyable it was to teach Bethany to care for the chickens and the other animals in the barn.

He felt protective over Tommy and looked

forward to spending time with him in the evenings, just rocking the small boy in the chair after supper until he fell asleep.

In just this short time, he realized that he wanted Gina, Bethany and Tommy to be a permanent part of his life. And if that meant marrying Gina, so be it.

How much of a hardship would it be?

She was beautiful, a wonderful cook, she cleaned his house and mended his clothes. In the springtime he'd clear an area for a garden. He would ask her on the ride home. Surely, she wouldn't deny him when his arms were around her. Even though it was too soon for her to feel anything towards him but gratitude, she must see that it was a wise choice for both her and the children.

When he arrived inside the mercantile, Ingrid was talking to Gina at the fabric counter. Ingrid's hands were moving in the air as she talked, while Gina listened with undivided attention. Joe was about to walk over, but he hesitated. Suddenly Gina gasped, and she burst into tears, pulling the older woman into a warm embrace.

Ingrid patted Gina on the back and pushed her away, before picking up her package from the counter, and patting Joe's arm as she walked past him to leave the store.

"You alright?" Joe asked, walking over to Gina.

She nodded. "Mrs. Chapman heard I was staying at the cabin. She offered me a job, so I don't have to worry about what I'm going to do after Christmas. It comes with a house and a small stipend."

"A job?"

"Yes. She needs help cooking and sewing for the cowboys at the ranch. She said there is another house on the property I'll be able to use. You'll have your house back." Gina was practically jumping up and down. "Isn't that exciting?" she choked, wiping the tears away from her cheeks. "This is the best Christmas ever."

Panic engulfed him. *A job? Moving?*

She looked so happy; he didn't dare tell her what was on his heart as they headed back home.

"Hmmm. Of course. The best Christmas ever."

CHAPTER NINE

Gina breathed a sigh of relief as the cabin came back into view. Joe was silent on the entire ride home. He held her, but there was something different in the way his arms wrapped around her. It was as if he was just keeping her steady on the horse.

She couldn't imagine what she did to make him upset with her. She was so excited at the prospect of being able to provide for herself and her children that she just jumped at what Mrs. Chapman offered.

Was that it?

Perhaps Joe didn't want her to leave.

Or did he have an issue with women working?

Oh goodness! That must be it!

Gina felt her stomach tighten.

Why that overbearing man, she thought! This isn't the 1700s!

If that was the case, then she would talk to Mrs. Chapman tomorrow at dinner and plan to move in as soon as possible. She wondered if Christmas Day would be too soon. Her shoulders slumped at the thought of having to pack up and move again. Even though they had only been at Joe's for just over a week, Gina loved everything about the little house.

She loved the great room with its gigantic fireplace. The window she could look out towards the barn. The privy wasn't too far from the back door, which was very nice in the frosty night air. She loved the small bedroom where she slept between the children in a bed not big enough to turn over in. She loved Joe checking in on her and coming over for dinner.

Oh, double goodness! That was it.

She loved Joe.

But how was that possible since she had only known him for such a short time?

It took her nearly a year to love David. Of course, she was fond of him before that, but she didn't feel anything akin to love. Why it took David nearly six weeks after the wedding to even kiss her!

How she felt about Joe was completely different. Not only was he a good man, but he was also a godly man. She couldn't recall David reading the Bible to the children after dinner. Gina ran down the list she had created earlier of his most endearing attributes in her mind once more. Wonderful kisser. Yes, she needed to add that to the list of attributes.

And if she was honest with herself, she wanted more of those kisses.

"We're home." Joe's husky voice broke through her thoughts. He walked Chestnut to the porch and guided Gina down from the horse's back.

The door cracked open, and Devin slipped outside. "You took longer than I expected."

"Sorry about that, brother," Joe said, dismounting Chestnut. "I found a flock of wild turkeys. I shot two of them."

"That's fantastic news! What are you going to do with them?"

"I'll clean one up for Christmas. The other I'll take over to Ma."

"If you give me my packages, I'll go inside and check on the children and start supper. I hope they weren't too much trouble."

Devin smiled. "Not at all. Tommy woke up. Bethany made him some soup and buttered bread. She taught me how to make bread." Giving Gina a wink, he took the packages from Joe. "She informed me I was kneading it wrong and made me practice until I got it correct."

Gina laughed. "She is rather bossy. Here, let me take those from you."

"I'll carry them inside. You look rather cold. I made a fresh pot of coffee. I can't promise it is still fresh, but at least it is hot."

Joe rummaged through his pocket and pulled out the bottle from Doc Mueller. "Here's Tommy's medicine. Doc said just a spoonful every four hours."

She took the bottle from Joe and held it close. "Thank you. Are you coming for dinner? I am just going to make eggs and toast."

Joe shook his head regretfully. "Not tonight. I have some things to do. I'll see you in the morning. Good night, Gina."

Gina dropped her face to hide her hurt. "Good night, Joe. Thank you for today."

Joe picked up Chestnut's lead and walked the horse toward the barn, whispering to it as they made their way across the yard. Devin gently kicked the door open with his foot and motioned for Gina to enter with his chin.

"Just ignore him. Let's get you inside before you catch a cold."

Giving a slight nod, Gina made her way inside the house. They had the kitchen table and floor covered in white, while the loaf pans rested under a towel. "It looks like a flour factory exploded."

"We didn't have time to clean up," Devin said sheepishly. He placed the packages on the chair next to the fireplace. "I'll get the flour wiped down."

"Where are the children?"

"Bethany was just here. Thomas went to lie back down."

Gina removed her wraps and draped them on the back of one of the kitchen chairs before unbuttoning the two shirts from Joe. She missed his scent, enveloping her. Hugging the shirt to her slightly, closing her eyes and inhaling, she reluctantly removed the shirt and added it to the pile of clothes. "I'll get it cleaned up right after I get a cup of coffee."

"Did something happen out there?"

Gina looked at Devin, who was staring at her. His observant eyes missed nothing as they traveled over her face, but she wouldn't betray her confidences of the day. "Why do you ask that?"

"I dunno. Joe would usually ask me to put the horse away and come get a cup of coffee. Or he'd put the horse away, ask me to go to Ma's and then come get a cup of coffee. I know he wouldn't turn down dinner unless there was a reason for it."

Her spirits sank even lower as the truth of Devin's words sounded hollow in her ears. "Maybe he had a reason for it." She grabbed a mug and moved to the coffeepot, which was warming over the fire.

Devin was silent for a moment, then he slapped his knee and gave a loud laugh. "He kissed you."

Gina nearly dropped her mug. "Shh. Do you want the children to hear you speak like that?"

Devin laughed even louder. "Ma said it's perfectly natural to want to kiss a woman and for a woman to want to kiss her man."

"Joe isn't my man."

"I think he is." Walking over to the pegs, he put on his hat and shrugged his arms into his coat before leaning down to give Gina a kiss on the cheek. "I think you'd be a fine wife and sister. I think Joe knows that as well."

Gina had just put the children to bed and was sitting by the fire, brushing her hair, when she heard the knock on the door. It was so faint she almost thought she imagined it.

Straining her ears, she tilted her head to see if she heard it again. There wasn't a knocking, but she heard movement on the porch. It was probably a raccoon rummaging for something to eat. Sighing, Gina put her brush aside and grabbed the broom, determined to shoo the critter away from the door. The noise sounded louder, as if the creature was moving to the far end of the porch.

Yanking the door open, Gina stepped outside, her bare toes curling under her nightgown from the bitter cold. "Alright, Mr. Racoon, there is nothing for you…" She stopped short as a shadow turned in the darkness and approached her.

Opening her mouth, she let loose such a shrill scream that it was sure to peel the skin back from the turkey carcasses hanging in the barn. She continued to shriek, praying that Joe or Devin might hear her. She glanced towards their cabin and saw a light through the window.

They must have heard. It would only take a few minutes for them to reach her door.

Backing into the cabin as quickly as possible, she held out the wooden end of the broom like a sword. "Stay back," she yelled at the shadow. "I have a rifle." Giving a little jab with the broom, she dropped it and pushed the door closed, lowering the bar across the door. "My husband will be back any minute."

Stupid, Gina. You shouldn't have mentioned that you were alone.

"Is he out hunting deer?" a muffled voice called through the door.

Her heart thundered in her chest, the roar of fear pounding in her ears. Gulping the air, she grabbed her nightgown, worrying the fabric with her hand. Thoughts raced through her head. *What was she going to do?* She hadn't been this scared since the people on the wagon train left her to survive on her own.

Survive on her own. She survived. She could survive. She calmed her breathing and leaned her head against the door, praying for whomever it was to go away.

"Go away." Her voice was so low she could barely hear it.

"Gina? It's me, sweetheart. It's just me."

"Joe?"

"Yes. It's Joe."

Gina lifted the bar and cracked open the door,

peeking outside. Joe stood on the porch with a lantern in his hand. A loud gasp escaped her lips. "What are you doing here? I thought you were a raccoon, then I thought... never mind." Opening the door, she pursed her lips. "You scared me to death, Joseph Moore."

"You thought what?" Joe rubbed the back of his neck, looking at her with glittering eyes.

Gina shifted uncomfortably, tugging at the neck of her nightgown. "I thought you were going to ravish me."

Joe laughed. "That's melodramatic. No. I'm not here to ravish you." He looked around at the line of trees, the moon casting their tall shadows into the clearing. "Can I come in? It is cold and I might perish if I stay out here a moment longer."

"*That's* very melodramatic. Of course, you can." Gina held open the door and moved aside to let Joe enter. "Can I get you some coffee?"

"I'd appreciate that." He put the lantern on the table and blew on his hands. "I was in such a rush to leave that I forgot my gloves."

"Stand by the fire and tell me why you are here at this hour. It's practically indecent."

"Yes, ma'am," he said, taking the mug and wrapping his hands around it. "Would you mind putting something else on?"

"Something else?" Gina looked down at her state of undress, her hand moved to cover herself. "Oh, my goodness!" Racing to the bedroom, she ducked inside, muttering about ungentlemanly callers who appear without warning. She pulled her day dress over her nightgown, and quickly did the buttons. It didn't matter to her if she was bulky or not. Joe wouldn't be staying very long. Adjusting the fabric to minimize looking like an overstuffed pillow, she returned to the great room and tried to pretend everything was normal.

He seemed to enjoy her struggle to remain calm. His eyes glittered as he looked at her, the twinkling speaking of some secret that she wasn't yet privy to. A muscle quivered near his jaw, and she watched his long fingers rub the offending spot. Her own fingers itched to brush his fingers away and trace the firm bone and touch his lips with her thumb. She needed to compose her thoughts before they completely ran away, and she couldn't control herself any longer.

She wasn't a wonton woman, but around Joe it appeared she lost all self-control. It would mortify her parents. It should mortify her. Silently reciting the Lord's Prayer, she felt a calmness settle over her.

"W-What do you want?" she finally asked.

He flipped his wrist, throwing the remains of his coffee into the fire. The wood hissed and sizzled as the liquid touched the embers. Dangling the mug off one finger, he gave it a little spin as he moved closer. She needed to remember he was a hunter, as she felt like prey caught in his sights.

"I came to see you." His voice was almost a purr.

Gina swallowed. "Well, here I am."

Putting the mug on the table, he crept around the table until he stood in front of her. He was so close she could count his eyelashes. His breath was warm on her cheeks. He lifted one finger and traced a line down her cheek. "Yes, you are. We have some unfinished business."

"We do?" She tried not to lean into his hand, and he cupped her face.

"Uh-huh."

"You need to tell Mrs. Chapman that you won't be going to work for her."

Gina's eyes snapped to his, and she lifted her head, immediately feeling the loss of his hand. Stepping away, her eyes narrowed slightly. "Why would I do that?"

"Because, as your husband, it would be my responsibility to provide for you."

"As my hus–" Gina's eyes opened with understanding. "Are you asking me to marry you?"

Joe nodded. "I was going to ask you on our way to town, but we found the birds. Then I was going to ask you on our way back from town, but you seemed so happy about leaving me."

"I wasn't happy about leaving you. I just thought you wanted your cabin back, and I knew you were going to talk to the Marshal about what to do."

"I never talked to the Marshal. There is nothing to do but marry me. That is your only option."

Gina lifted one eyebrow. "My only option?"

"Uh-huh. I wasn't happy when I thought about you leaving. You don't want to take care of all those cowboys."

"I don't?" Her eyes flew open. "You were?"

"I wasn't happy at all. In fact, I was downright disappointed that Marmee even said something."

"She was just trying to help, I'm sure of it."

"Perhaps. In her own way."

Joe moved closer. Gina walked backwards, bumping into the table. Feeling her way around it, she moved towards the far wall. Joe continued to stalk her, like the hunter he was.

"You don't think so?"

"When Ingrid Chapman gets an idea in her head, nothing will stop her."

Placing her hands behind her, Gina felt the edge of the wall. Her fingers inched along until her back rested on the logs. Joe grinned as he leaned over her. His hands rested on the wall, boxing her in. One hand was just inches from her head, the other nearer her waist. She was trapped, but fear was replaced with anticipation.

She hoped he was going to kiss her. He leaned down, his face a few inches from hers. Gina swallowed hard, her lips parting slightly. "What idea did she get?"

Joe grinned, like a predator going in for the kill. "That we should get married."

"I don't recall her saying that."

"It wasn't what she said. It was what she didn't say." He lowered his head to kiss next to her ear. "Tell me you'll marry me, Gina. Stay here at the cabin with me."

Her fingers pushed off from the wall and gripped his shoulders, turning her head just slightly so he could trace her neck with his nose. "You need to ask me first."

Joe pulled back suddenly, and his expression stilled. Gina released his shoulders.

Perhaps she had behaved too wantonly.

Joe was a godly man, but even a godly man has his limits.

"Joe. I-I."

"Shh." He grabbed her hand and walked her to the kitchen table. Pulling out one chair, he sat down, lowering her onto his knee. "You are correct. I didn't do this the right way. Gina Graham, will you do me the honor of being my bride? Of letting me love you all the days of my life? Will you let me love your children as my own?"

"Oh, Joe!" Gina threw her arms around his neck and kissed his face. "Yes. I will marry you. I never thought I'd find love again, but God has brought me to you."

"We'll get married tomorrow when Reverend O'Brien performs the Christmas Eve service. After that, I will ravish you," he teased, wiggling his eyebrows.

"But Joe, I don't have anything to wear."

"Don't worry, my love. I had Rose pick out a dress for you and Bethany. She also picked out a pair of pants and a shirt for Thomas." He took her face gently in his large hand and pulled her closer. "You thrill me, Gina. I love you and I thank God for leading me to you that day." Tilting his head, he captured her lips, sending shivers of delight through her.

When they finally broke apart, they were both half-laughing, half crying. Joe wiped Gina's tears away with his thumbs. The sound of giggles caused their attention to turn to the bedroom door. It quickly closed, and they heard the children scampering to get back in bed.

Thomas's raspy voice carried from behind the thin wood. "Didn't I tell you, Beth? We got a Pa for Christmas."

CHAPTER TEN

"You may now kiss the bride."

Joe didn't hesitate to pull Gina into his arms, and his mouth swooped down to capture hers. Her knees went weak, limp under the pleasure of his kiss, but he held her, consumed with the promise that he would never let her fall.

Her fingers made their way up his arms and curled around his biceps, clinging to the fabric of his jacket. Joe blocked out everything but the woman beneath him. He felt a hand slap him on the back and was about to make his displeasure known when he heard the calls of everyone in the barn celebrating all the marriages.

Four couples were married in the large barn, with Reverend O'Brien presiding over the ceremony and most of Flat River's residents in attendance.

"Congrats, brother," Devin said, slapping Joe once more on the shoulder. "And welcome to the family, Gina." He grabbed Gina and swung her around in a hug before dropping her to the floor. "I knew he wouldn't let you go."

Joe and Gina were soon caught up with the other couples as townsfolk made their way around, congratulating the new couples and providing advice for a helpful marriage. Finally, Joe and Gina could take a quick break to sign Reverend O'Brien's book and find the children. Bethany was playing with a cornhusk doll the Chapmans gave to each of the girls, while Tommy was watching Joe's nephew Percy play with his new slingshot. Percy even let Tommy have a go, trying to hit the side of a milk pail with a small rock.

Tommy let Percy play with his wooden cup and ball game. The object was to catch a ball fastened to a handle by a string by tossing it into the cup.

Percy gave up rather quickly and wanted his slingshot back.

Once everyone had signed the register and Reverend O'Brien said the blessing for the food, they sat and ate a marvelous feast of venison, goose, wild onions, pickles, buttered bread, and every kind of cake, cookie, and pie imaginable.

Weston Chapman read from the Book of Luke, describing the Nativity, and his wife led everyone in singing *Silent Night*. Afterwards Verna Hartman, one of the other neighbors, read from the book of Matthew, and a resounding chorus of *Joy to the World* could be heard from the barn.

Soon the sun was setting in the sky, and Joe knew he needed to get his family home. Gathering up Tommy, who was coughing again, he bundled up his son in his new coat and carried him to the wagon filled with supplies.

"What's all this?" Gina asked.

"I ordered everything when we went to the store yesterday. I just asked Dillon to bring it to me today."

"You return the wagon to the livery when you can, Joe. No rush," Dillon called, as he wrapped his arm around Rose and headed to the long table to grab another piece of pie.

"Where's Bethany?" Joe asked.

"She's right here." Ingrid walked over, holding Bethany and Alice's hand. "I think Bethany had a lovely time. She's more than welcome to come visit once the weather turns warmer. I hope you feel better, Tommy. You need to go to bed as soon as you get home."

"I will Marmee! Thank you for my game."

"You're welcome." Opening her arms to Gina, Ingrid embraced the new bride. "I'm so glad you are here in Flat River. Once the ground softens, we can discuss your garden over a cup of tea."

"I'd like that very much."

Joe helped Bethany into the wagon, making sure she and Tommy were tucked in securely between the bags of flour and sugar. Once Gina finished saying her goodbyes to the Chapmans and Joe's family, he helped her onto the front of the wagon before climbing up beside her.

With a wave, he started the wagon on the slow ride back to their home.

Gina moved over, tucking her hand under his arm and leaning her head on his shoulder.

"Pa?"

Joe's heart burst with the one word.

"Yes, Tommy?"

"This was the best Christmas ever."

Joe reached his arm around his wife and pulled her closer, before putting his hand in the back of the wagon and capturing Tommy's hand in his own. He felt Bethany's small hand lay on top of his.

"It was," Joe agreed.

"I love you, Pa." Bethany said, patting his hand.

His voice, thick with emotion, could barely choke out the words. "I love you, too." He looked at Gina, who was smiling at him, her eyes glossy with unshed tears. "I love you, Gina."

"I love you, Joe," she said, rubbing her head on his arm.

"Hey, Pa?" Tommy said, releasing Joe's hand.

"What is it, buddy?"

"Will you teach me to hunt? I want to be just

like you."

"You got it. Once you are feeling better, we'll do it together."

"I'm glad we got a Pa for Christmas, aren't you Bethany?"

Joe wrapped his arm around Gina's shoulders and looked at the stars twinkling in the night as the children chattered on the back of the wagon. They might be thankful that they received a father for Christmas, but Joe was thankful to his Father in Heaven that he received a family.

One year later

Gina pulled the Dutch oven from the fireplace and lifted the lid. The biscuits were a perfect golden color. Giving the skillet gravy a final stir, she pulled the spider skillet away from the coals to let it cool for a few minutes.

"Merry Christmas, sweetheart."

She shifted on her heels to see her husband walking towards her. She couldn't believe they had been married a year and a day, and her feelings hadn't diminished one bit since the moment she first saw him.

He ran his fingers through his uncombed hair before stretching his arms in the air and yawning.

Gina rolled back to a standing position and carried the biscuit pan to the table before turning to stand in front of him. Lifting her arms around his neck, she pulled him down until her lips were inches from his face.

"Good morning, darling. Merry Christmas," she said, leaning up on her toes to press a quick kiss against her husband's firm lips.

His arms wrapped around her waist, pulling her hard against him. He pressed a gentle kiss against her forehead. "Have I told you today how much I love you?"

Gina giggled. "No. You just woke up, silly."

He lifted his hand to tuck a wayward strand of hair behind her ear. "I love you very much, Mrs. Moore."

"I love you too. More than I ever knew possible."

With another quick kiss, he released her and fetched a cup of coffee. "Did Devin say he was coming over?"

Gina pulled the biscuits out of the Dutch oven and put them in a basket, covering them with a cloth to keep them warm. "He didn't, but I made enough just in case."

Taking a sip from his mug, he sat down at the table and patted his knee for her to take a set. "I can't believe the children aren't awake yet."

"They were plumb tuckered out from the party yesterday."

"I think the Chapmans outdid themselves this year."

"Let me get your breakfast before it gets cold."

"I have a little something for you." He walked over to the tree and pulled out two small packages from between the branches.

"Joe, I thought we decided we weren't going to do anything."

He shrugged his shoulders. "It's just something small."

"Should I wait until the children wake up?"

He placed the packages on the table, and lifting her hand, he kissed her knuckles. "No. Let's just enjoy this quiet moment."

"I have a gift for you, too, Joe."

Joe lifted his eyebrow. "I thought we agreed, no presents."

Gina laughed. "Well, I didn't actually spend anything."

"Okay, well, you open yours while I eat."

Gina held his hand as her husband asked for a blessing over the food and watched as he helped himself to several biscuits, covering them with thick gravy. He picked up her plate and put a smaller portion on it before sliding it in front of her.

Taking the first gift, Gina carefully pulled the string and removed the paper.

"Oliver Twist by Charles Dickens. How wonderful, Joe."

"I thought it might be something we could read to the children in the evenings. After the Bible, of course."

"Of course." Picking up the smaller box, she

gave it a little shake. The box rattled. "I wonder what it is?" Shaking it once more, she smiled. "Is it a rock?" Joe laughed. "A penny?"

"Would you just open it, woman. Your breakfast is going to get cold."

"I want to savor the moment." Opening the package, her eyes snapped to Joe's as she picked out a simple gold band from within the box. "It's a ring."

"I didn't get you a wedding ring last year since we got married so quickly. Dillon ordered it, but it took forever to arrive. Can you believe it's been nearly a year?"

"Oh Joe, you didn't need to do that."

"Yes, I did." Curling his fingers, he held his hand towards her. "Give it to me." Placing the ring in his palm, she smiled. "With this ring, I thee wed," he said, repeating the words of the preacher from the previous year. Sliding the ring over Gina's knuckle, he curled her fingers under and kissed the ring and smiled at her, a devilish look coming into his eyes. "Maybe the children will sleep longer?" he said, wiggling his eyebrows.

"Joseph Moore, you are incorrigible." Weaving

her fingers through his dark hair, she pulled him closer for a kiss. His mouth covered hers hungrily, and she found herself lost in his kiss. When she finally pulled away, it took a moment for her thoughts to line up. "I like it when you are incorrigible."

Joe threw back his head and laughed. "Only for you, my love." Picking up another biscuit to sop in his gravy, he looked at her. "Now, you said you had something for me?"

Sliding from her seat, she moved towards him. Pushing the hair back from his eyes, she stood over him and smiled. *Would there ever be a day when she didn't crave his touch?* She certainly hoped not.

Taking his hand, she placed it on her belly and grinned. "I went to see the Doc this week. Our family will expand in the summer."

Joe dropped his fork and stood, pulling Gina into a tight embrace, swinging her around the room, before easing her down to the floor. "Really? Oh, my goodness, you need to sit down. Don't you worry, I'll get someone to help you. What do you need? Here, have some more food." He started piling more biscuits on Gina's plate. "You can have mine."

"Joe, honestly. Women have been having babies, well, since before you were born. I'll be fine. Doc said I'm healthy and there should be no reason the baby isn't either. Aren't you excited?"

He kissed the top of her head. "You do not know."

"Did you tell him, Ma?" Bethany said, rushing into the room with Tommy on her heels.

"Yeah, did you tell Pa?" Tommy came over and wrapped his arms around Joe's legs.

"She sure did."

Gina thought she saw Joe wipe tears away from his eyes.

Suddenly, the door crashed open, and a gust of wind burst into the room.

"Uncle Devin!" Tommy cried, rushing over to grab the door. "Merry Christmas!"

"Merry Christmas, Tommy," Devin said, pushing his way into the room. "Merry Christmas, Bethany. Brother, Gina. Look what I shot this morning up on the ridge." He held up a large Tom turkey. "What a feast this will be. I had to clean it which is why I was late."

"Ma's having a baby," Bethany said.

Devin looked at Joe, his eyes opening in surprise. "Congratulations, Joe, that's wonderful. Gina, how are you feeling?"

"A little tired, but wonderful. Let me take the turkey and I'll get it ready for supper. Merry Christmas, Devin." She kissed her brother-in-law on the cheek and took the turkey and put it in a clean pot. "Wash your hands and breakfast is ready."

After a delicious breakfast of biscuits, gravy, jam and coffee, the children opened their presents. Bethany was thrilled with her own leather sewing kit filled with needles and pins, along with a yard of fabric and some thread. Tommy received a small knife so he could learn woodworking, and a spinning top. Each received a brand-new shiny cup of their own. Uncle Devin brought them a small sack of gumdrops, which they put away to savor.

Joe started reading the book of Luke as Gina prepared dinner, the children and Devin hanging on his every word as Joe recounted the tale of

Christ's birth. They snacked on meats and cheeses, and pickles and cookies while they waited for the turkey to be done.

By the time it was dark, dinner was done, and the children were fast asleep on the floor with full bellies and full hearts. Devin said goodnight and made his way back to his cabin under the full moon.

As they watched Devin walk across the barnyard and slip inside to check on the animals, Joe wrapped his arms around his wife, pulling her back against his chest. The soft whiskers of his beard tickled her cheek.

"We should get the children to bed," Gina whispered.

"I'll carry them to bed shortly. Let's just stand out here for a moment." Gina leaned back in her husband's arms, relishing the feel of them around her. Looking out at the clear sky, she could count the stars if she wanted to. The air was frosty, but she didn't feel any of it. She knew if Joe was next to her, she'd always be warm.

He rubbed his chin against her. "Did you have a good Christmas, my love?" he asked softly.

"I did. You?"

His hand slid down to her slightly rounded belly and cupped it gently. "I did."

"This is my favorite time of year," she said, looking back over her shoulder.

Joe moved his hand and lifted her chin with two fingers, caressing her lips softly. "Mine too. It was when my life changed forever."

"How's that?" she murmured against his mouth.

"It was when I found my Christmas bride."

I hope you enjoyed Joe and Gina's story! Look for Devin's story kicking off a brand-new series called Flat River Blessings, launching in Fall 2023.

Be sure to check out the next book in the First Families of Flat River with NOT HIS MAIL-ORDER BRIDE, featuring Weston and Ingrid's oldest son, Owen Chapman. I hope you continue the adventure with the Chapman Family and all the settlers in Flat River, Nebraska.

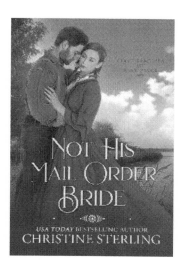

To find out more about this book, the First Families of Flat River series, its characters, and all the series set in this lovely fictional town, visit www.flatrivernebraska.com.

About Christine Sterling

USA Today bestselling author **CHRISTINE STERLING** writes small-town inspirational romances with a touch of humor. Most of her stories take place in the plains of Nebraska or Colorado, but she will write wherever there are cowboys needing to find love. Her favorite stories involve tight-knit families, and you will often find that her characters cross over in many of her stories.

She lives on a farm in Pennsylvania with her husband, four dogs, and one spoiled cat, aka The Floof. She can often be found in her garden with a notebook and a cup of tea.

FOLLOW ME ON SOCIAL MEDIA

BookBub

https://www.bookbub.com/authors/christine-sterling

Join Christine's Chatters Reader Group

https://www.facebook.com/groups/148223709303134

Visit my Website

https://www.christinesterling.com

Made in the USA
Middletown, DE
14 December 2024

67019304R00092